I Am Scrooge

I Am Scrooge

A Zombie Story for Christmas

By Adam Roberts

with illustrations by Zom Leech

Copyright © Adam Roberts 2009
All rights reserved

The right of Adam Roberts to be identified as the author
of this work has been asserted by him in accordance with the
Copyright, Designs and Patents Act 1988.

First published in Great Britain in 2009 by Gollancz
An imprint of the Orion Publishing Group
Orion House, 5 Upper St Martin's Lane,
London WC2H 9EA
An Hachette UK Company

This edition published in Great Britain in 2012 by Gollancz

A CIP catalogue record for this book
is available from the British Library

ISBN 978 0 575 09490 1

1 3 5 7 9 10 8 6 4 2

Typeset by Input Data Services Ltd,
Bridgwater, Somerset

Printed and bound by CPI Group (UK) Ltd,
Croydon, CRO 4YY

The Orion Publishing Group's policy is to use papers
that are natural, renewable and recyclable products and
made from wood grown in sustainable forests. The logging
and manufacturing processes are expected to conform to
the environmental regulations of the country of origin.

www.adamroberts.com
www.orionbooks.co.uk

PREFACE

I have endeavoured in this Zombic little book, to decapitate the Zombie of an Idea, which I trust shall devour my readers' brains, and pursue them shudderingly yet persistently along the street. But in a good way. May it thump upon the boarded-up windows of their houses pleasantly, and no one wish to remake it as a major motion picture starring Will Smith.

Your faithful Friend and Servant,
A. R. R. R. R.
December 1843

Marley's Zombie

Marley was dead, to begin with. Dead for about three minutes, that is: then he got up again. The clergyman, the clerk and the undertaker had all certified him dead; and these were all men experienced in the business of dealing with dead bodies. They were all astonished, then – and more than astonished – to hear his corpse groan and to see it shake and move. If their surprise did not last long, it was only because it very quickly turned to terror as Marley reached out, sank his fingers into the soft flesh of the clerk's and the undertaker's throats, and, using them as leverage, pulled himself forward to bite down hard into the face of the clergyman. The churchman's nose was bulbous and red, a fleshy appendage, but Marley bit into it as eagerly as if it had been a ripe strawberry. He hauled the three men together in a grisly group-embrace: clerk and undertaker croaking and scrabbling ineffectually at Marley's grip pulled tight into the clergyman's back, preventing that reverend gentleman from withdrawing from the horror and agony that was happening to his face. With more than human force his teeth drove and chewed, ripping away flesh – the face now a slick mess of red, but the flowing blood only lubricated Marley's grinding progress. From the clergyman's open mouth came a scream that issued as fierce and high-pitched as a steam whistle – though he wriggled and fought with an energy he had not displayed in his life for many years, he could not escape. Marley's teeth tore away the flesh of the face and reached the skull beneath it uncovering those two gaps in the bone shaped like tear drops that underlie the nose. Marley bit hard, and cracked through to the marrow – so violently, indeed, that one of his yellow front teeth broke away and lodged in the corner of the clergyman's eye socket. But he had reached what he sought – the soft brain matter. Thrusting forward he chomped mouthfuls of this substance and swallowed, working his way through the churchman's frontal lobes. At this grisly progress the victim's screeching ceased. His arms fell limp. For moments he remained alive, and even conscious after a fashion, though blinded and muti-lated, as the very substance of his self was bolted down mouth-ful by mouthful. Shortly his skull was emptied, as an egg is sucked clean of its meat. Marley leant back – his own face smeared in gore and tightened his grip on the two throats he held. His fingernails met through the flesh: he raised his arms, holding a bleeding lump of matter in each fist, and two bodies fell away to thump upon the floor. There lay the clerk and undertaker of this parish, their white faces clenched in ricti of terror.

The clock finished chiming the hour: just turned midnight.

That which had, in life, been Marley turned to the door. A growl escaped his throat, something between a groan and a word:

'Scrooooooge . . .'

Who owned the name into which Marley's Zombie had inserted so many superogatory 'o's? Ebeneezer Scrooge, that is who. Scrooge sat in his counting-house – his place of work, and so-called because, after years of wheeler-dealing, and dealing things more lucrative even than wheels, he was now indeed wealthy enough to count his houses. He didn't live in the houses he counted, of course. They were merely collateral for his financial deals. But he owned a good number.

It was cold, bleak, biting weather: and foggy too, a strange brown miasma that smelled of foulness. Scrooge could hear the people in the court outside go wheezing up and down, beating their hands upon their breasts, and stamping their feet upon the pavement stones to warm them. And Scrooge wheezed too – for who could breath properly in so foul a reek? As the night began to freeze, and he was a right wheezer, and he went by the name of Ebeneezer Scrooge.

What sort of a person was he? Ah, as the phrase goes, thereby hangs a tale! Not hangs in the public execution sense; that wouldn't be appropriate at all, in this context. I mean *hangs* in the – well, now. To be honest, I'm not entirely sure in what sense a tale can be said to *hang*. What I mean is that there was a reason behind Scrooge's poor public reputation.

People said that he was as tight-fisted as a hand at the gravestone, Scrooge – a squeezing, wrenching, grasping, scraping, clutching, covetous old miser. That's what they said. Hard and sharp as flint, from which no steel had ever struck out generous fire; secret, and self-contained, and solitary as an oyster. Hurtful stuff, really. But that is how people are; they rarely think the effect their words will have on the insides of the people whose outsides may – I say *may* – be a *touch* on the squeezing, wrenching, grasping, scraping, clutching, covetous old miserly side. And nobody ever spoke up for Scrooge's good qualities: his excellent punctuality, for instance. His bookkeeping skills – not enough people share those. Nor did people give Scrooge credit for his *sang-froid*. It rarely came up in conversation, although the truth of the matter is that nobody's *sang* was *froider*.

People said that Scrooge's heart was three sizes too small. Too small!

It is not clear what they meant, since there was nothing wrong with Scrooge's circulation. The organ in question was, after all, large enough to pump blood through Scrooge's body. Which was its job. We might wonder: in what sense *too small*? Did the people who said so have plans to – in some sense – *wear* the organ in question, themselves? But to be frank, it is not clear to me why anybody would want to. Wear it *in what capacity*? That's the question nobody is answering! It could, I suppose, and at a pinch, be used as a boxing glove. It would be considerably more than three sizes too small to be a hat. But in either case the main objection would not be one of size, but general efficacy – the scarlet wetness would stain, the fabric would be of limited use. Let us, on balance, spend no longer on the actual size of Scrooge's heart.

Had Scrooge always been an antisocial, miserly sort? By no means! By *no* means! By no *means*! OK, the middle one, I think.

Scrooge – even Scrooge – had once been a blithe and cheery lad, as open-hearted and giddy with joy as any. But something had happened to change him. One Christmas Eve many years before, a cheery lad had been coming home from school, full of the freedom of the holidays, and the excitement of the coming Christmas Day. Nine years old and each of those years filled with the joy and hope, the energy and curiosity of youth. His path from school to his home took him though the grounds of a church – but although this meant walking alongside the graves, and although it was a dark and misty evening, he had not been afraid. He had walked this same path a thousand times.

But this one time it had been different: young Scrooge had been the victim of an unprovoked and unsettling assault. A scarecrow figure – ghastly, old, and rank with an unnatural smell – had leapt upon him. He had seized the young boy, shaken him, shouted in his face, and then – worst of all – stabbed him in the arm with a thin blade. The physical wound was superficial, and in truth little more than a scratch that healed in a few days. But the wound to young Scrooge's self-assurance, to his mind, was much deeper. The shock scared the lad half to death and sufficiently out of his wits that, when he came back to them, he discovered he had lost his former blitheness. Fellow-feeling was replaced now by caution and suspicion. From that day, and because of that attack, he had grown increasingly sour and reclusive with each passing year.

On such hinges do lives turn about.

And now here he was, in late middle age, in his counting-house. Though the rest of the world was readying itself for Christmas, that was a day, and a festival, with only unpleasant associations to him.

The city clocks chimed three, but the afternoon was quite dark already – it had not been light all day – and candles were flaring in the windows of the neighbouring offices, like ruddy smears upon the palpable brown air. The fog came pouring in at every chink and keyhole, and was so dense without, that although the court was of the narrowest, the houses opposite were mere phantoms. To see the dingy cloud come drooping down, obscuring everything, one might have thought that some fissure had opened in the geologic barrier between mortal life and Hell itself, and the breath of something inarticulable, something ancient and implacable, was seeping through.

Something was amiss in London Town, and its inhabitants slunk from the shadows, and whispered to one another that monstrous things were lurking in the East End. Fear stalked the city like a giant, er, stork.

The apprehension penetrated even into the matter-of-fact den of Scrooge and Marley. And, yes, although it had been many years since Ebeneezer Scrooge and Nathan Marley had parted company, Scrooge had been too miserly to have the sign over his doorway repainted: Scrooge and Marley's, it still said. Fear crept through the air like a miasma. Even Scrooge felt it, although he ignored the feeling. He lived to work, and so he worked even late into this chilly Christmas Eve. The holiday meant nothing to him.

His clerk, Terence Cratchit, felt it more acutely than most for he was a timid, shrinking little soul. He sat in the front room of Scrooge's counting-house, and his master occupied the back room. From time to time Scrooge called his clerk through for some task or other, and Cratchit stood shivering. 'Are you ill sir?'

'No, Mr Scrooge.'

'Cold then?'

'It is cold – but it's not that, sir.'

'What?'

'Rumours, sir. Bad, bad, bad intimations. Some malign evil is seeping through the foggy streets this very night, sir.'

'Bah!' coughed Scrooge, for the fog got in his throat and agitated a slight tracheal infection from which he suffered. But although his reputation was one of utter inhumanity, he wasn't such a sour old puss. He even felt a certain sympathy for his trembling clerk. 'Hmm,' he pondered aloud. Then an objection occurred to him. 'Bu—' he started to say, before another cough 'kh!' caught in his gullet.

'I'm sorry, Mr Scrooge?'

'I,' said Scrooge, clearing his throat: 'I was going to say: but tomorrow is Christmas! Hmm, hmm. Surely you are looking forward to that?'

'My *kids* are, sir,' said Cratchit, his face lightening a little. 'Little George and Georgina, and littlest Georgia too. And Tiny Tim, bless his heart. We've legally adopted him now, sir, so he's officially part of the family! Although he's so sick it worries Mrs Cratchit something shocking.'

'Isn't adoption a rather expensive business?' queried Scrooge. 'I mean – extending your family?'

'He needs looking after, the poor crippled fellow,' said Cratchit.

'It sounds like *you* need looking after,' said Scrooge, in a severe voice. 'Trembling with fear?'

'I'll confess it, sir, I'm frightened to walk home tonight!'

'You could take a – bah! – hmm!' Scrooge coughed, 'buggy?'

'That would be more than my pocket could manage, sir.'

This smelt to Scrooge rather of a man angling for a handout, which in turn piqued his suspicious, stand-offish nature. He sent the clerk back to work and settled down to finishing off his own bookkeeping.

'Scary Christmas, Uncle!' cried a voice, at the main door. It was the voice of Scrooge's nephew, and, as is the way with human voices, it was not unaccompanied by the man himself. In stepped nephew Fred a moment later.

'What is it, Nephew?' Scrooge demanded.

'A foul night, Uncle – something amiss in London Town!'

'Bah!' coughed Scrooge, covering his mouth.

'The fog,' said Fred, in a knowing voice. 'Not good for the

respiration. And there are rumours of some terrible, mur-derous evil abroad. There's death in the air. Have you heard about Marley?'

'What about old Marley?'

'At death's door, they're saying. Won't last the night, that's what I heard.'

'That'll put an end to his charitable giving,' observed Scrooge, stony-faced.

Fred laughed. 'You never did like his being so charitably disposed!'

'I didn't mind his wasting his own money on that nonsense,' Scrooge observed. 'I simply objected him to using the *firm's* money. That's the reason we parted company.'

'His name's still over the door, I see?'

'I must,' Scrooge muttered, 'get round to repainting that.'

'Well he'll soon be dead. The word is all round the city – attended by doctors. Death's in the air. On Christmas Eve too!' A sly look came over Fred's face. 'Not a night to be walking home, I'd say.'

'And how am I to get home if I don't walk?' said Scrooge, irritably.

'You could come with *me*,' said his nephew, smiling a self-satisfied smile, and reaching forward and taking hold of the sleeve of his uncle's coat. 'I happen to have a closed carriage outside—'

'A carriage?' retorted Scrooge, sharply. 'And how can you afford such indulgence?'

'I know! Swanky, isn't it? Swank-*eee*.'

'You've not really come to offer me a lift,' said Scrooge, with a grim expression. 'You've come to show off.'

'It's top of the range – white-wall cartwheels, bronze cabs on the hubs, and go-canter stripes down the side! Hay injec-tion engine. Do you want to come and have a look?'

'I'm too busy for that,' Scrooge snapped.

'Please yourself. I'd like to invite you round for Christmas dinner tomorrow, Uncle; but, as you and I both know, Hilda can't stand the sight of you. So I shan't be seeing you until after the festivities. Good night, and season's greetings! Have a care walking home through the fog and the rumoured flesh-eating monsters.'

At this, Cratchit let out a little 'eek!' noise and rose trem-blingly from his high stool. 'Sir,' he quavered, crisply. 'Your splendid-sounding closed carriage . . . ?'

Scrooge's nephew paused at the door. 'What's that, fellow?'

'Would it be . . . might there be . . . ?' the quivering clerk pressed.

'Spit it out, man.'

'I live in the Borough, sir, and it is a long walk through – as you say sir – dangerous streets . . .'

Scrooge's nephew peered at the diminutive figure. 'I'm not following, my good man.'

At this Scrooge barked with laughter. 'Ha! Bah! Ha! That offer you made to me of a ride in the carriage! He asks you to match it – to match it for Cratchit.'

'Ah,' said Scrooge's nephew's face, an expression of com-prehension being quickly followed by one of disgust. 'Ah, I, eh— Borough, you say? I'm afraid my house is in quite another direction. Good night to you both. And Uncle?'

'Good night, Nephew,' said Scrooge.

'And I only pray,' said Fred, as a parting shot – and still hoping to get a rise out of his uncle, 'that the horror stalking this city *spares* you, this yuletide.'

'A spare-y Christmas to you too,' Scrooge retorted.

Finally, as the darkness thickened, and the poor took wing to their rookeries of wood, Scrooge shut up his shop. It was Christmas Eve, and though he was happy to work through the whole season – for what was Christmas to him? – his customers were less assiduous. The money he had lent would wait until Boxing Day; the stocks he had purchased and bonds he had acquired would sit in his strong-box until then.

'You can lock up, Cratchit,' said Scrooge, finally.

'Yes, sir.'

He stepped out, and the office was closed behind him in a twinkling (for the clerk preferred not to be alone longer than he had to). As Scrooge stomped away, Cratchit ran home to Southwark as hard as he could pelt, as if the Devil himself were on his heels.

As for Scrooge, he was wrapped up in comforter and great-coat, and he tucked his chin down as he walked. The fog and darkness had thickened still further, as if a dark and ominous cloud had given up its dream of flight and was rubbing its serpentine belly upon the ground. The ancient bell tower of a local church, invisible now, struck the hours and quarters in the murk with tremulous vibrations afterwards as if its teeth were chattering in its frozen head. The cold became intense. In the main street, at the corner of the court, some labourers were repairing the gas-pipes, and had lighted a great fire in a brazier; but no party of ragged men and boys gathered there to warm their hands before the blaze, and the workmen them-selves looked anxiously about as if afeared that some terror would lurch from the fog at any moment. The water-plug being left in solitude, its overflowings sullenly congealed, and turned to misanthropic ice, resembled cream about the lip of a cream jug.

The opacity of the air muffled sound; footsteps loomed in and out of hearing, although neither feet nor the bodies perched upon them could be seen. He passed a row of shops, their windows lit and Christmas wares on display; but the shoppers had stayed away, and the owners stood nervously in the doorways, debating with themselves whether the possibility of one extra sale outweighed the danger that murderers might be lurking. One homeless urchin, shivering in too scant a set of clothes, stood before a lit Butcher's window singing a Christmas carol:

> *God rest you, merry gentleman!*
> *Let nothing you display!*

He held out a hand as Scrooge passed, but his naked wrists and ankles, gnawed and mumbled by the hungry cold as bones are gnawed by dogs, only raised anger in the old miser's chest. He shooed the beggar away and quickened his pace.

Foggier yet, and colder. At one point Scrooge thought he heard a cry of terror, or pain, emerging from the murk – the sound of somebody's last breath leaving their chest at full force. It brought Fred's mocking words to his mind, and he halted; but after a moment of casting about himself, and seeing nothing in the mist, he started again. 'Old fool,' he told himself, coughing a little in the fog. 'I'll be, bah! hum! buggered if I get all jumpy at nothing but shadows and mist.'

But he couldn't prevent the fear from seeping into his thoughts. He made his way through the Aldwych as nervously as if an Old Witch still lived there, and was just lengthening his stride along the Strand – coming closer to his home now – when a strange thing happened. He heard a man call his name: 'Scrooge! Ebeneezer Scrooge!'

Scrooge stopped, and turned, and saw – although the fog and the dark made it hard to be certain – himself. At the very least it was a man who looked very like himself; and he was standing beside the vacant tollbooth at the head of Southwark bridge wearing a nightgown, bedsocks and nightcap. Hardly the best clothing for such freezing weather. He was waving his arms, and hollooing: 'Scroooge!'

Scrooge paused, startled into anger. He turned to face the fellow. 'Do you *know* me sir?'

'Scrooge!' the stranger called out! 'Beware!'

Already irritable with fear and cold, this pushed Scrooge over the edge. 'Oh *go off* sir,' he barked in return. 'Go *away*. Go on your way.'

'Beware of Marley!' the stranger bellowed. 'When you get home remember—'

The second person to mention Marley that evening. 'Remember what?' Something about this encounter – some eerie quality it possessed – made Scrooge's marrow shudder somewhat inside his bones. 'Get a grip,' he told himself.

The other fellow was evidently feeling the chill – as well he might, dressed as he was – his teeth chattered as he added: 'To be per-properly *pre*pared, p-p-p-pick up a *poker*.'

This strange allocution finally struck sparks of fear in Scrooge's breast. What was the fellow saying? Was he about to attack *him* with a poker? He was certainly coming closer. Scrooge braced himself for attack.

'Go *off*, sir!' Scrooge insisted.

'I can help you,' the strange man yelled. There was something disconcerting about his appearance – as if Scrooge had known this man, once, a long time ago. 'Listen to what I have to tell you,' called the stranger. 'You can bash his head in with a poker – take hold of the poker! No, wait – *don't* take hold of the poker . . .'

'Take hold? Don't take hold? What are you *on about*, sir?'

'Think if you possess an *oven glove!*' the stranger demanded. 'Wait. Do *I* possess an oven glove? I can't remember!'

Scrooge took a step back. 'You are insane!'

'The way to kill him,' said the stranger, increasingly agitated, 'is to put all the gold in your strong-box *into your chest of drawers!*'

'That'll kill him, will it? This is *gibberish!*' roared Scrooge. 'Do you take me for a fool? You're a lunatic, escaped from an asylum! And,' he added, feeling courage pour through him, 'don't think of attacking *me* – by putting gold into my drawers, or any other means.'

'A *gold bar!*' boomed the fellow.

'Bar? Humbug!' Scrooge shook his fist. 'So that's it, is it? You mean to rob the gold bar from out of my strong-box, do you? I'll defend it to the death. You'll not get my gold! Any attempt to come at *me*, and you'll catch it, sir. You'll catch it, then! Assuredly!'

This seemed to discourage the fellow; and briskly too, for he turned on his heels and began a lumbering sprint past the unmanned tollbooth and across the bridge.

Scrooge stood for a moment, and then resumed his walk home. Christmas, he thought to himself. Drunk, probably, he thought to himself. One more reason to dislike the season. Scrooge took a principled objection to liquor; the principle in question one of cost rather than intoxication, but a principle nevertheless.

Finally, Scrooge turned into a gloomy, deserted court and opened the main door to his chambers. He lived in a set of rooms that had once belonged to his partner, Marley: a gloomy suite, in a lowering pile of building mostly given over to commercial lets. The yard was so dark that even Scrooge, who knew its every stone, was fain to grope with his hands. The fog and frost so hung about the black old gateway of the house, that it seemed as if the Genius of the Weather had coated the whole in a chilling glittery paint.

Scrooge opened the main door; and when he was inside slammed it behind him. The sound resounded through the house like thunder. Every room above, and every cask in the wine-merchant's cellars below, appeared to have a separate peal of echoes of its own. But Scrooge, as he lit a candle from the alcove in at the doorway, was not a man to be frightened by echoes. He walked across the hall, and up the stairs, slowly too, trimming his candle as he went.

Half a dozen gas-lamps out of the street wouldn't have lighted the entry too well, so you may suppose that it was pretty dark with Scrooge's single trembling flame. Up Scrooge went, not caring a button for that. Darkness is cheap, and Scrooge liked that about it. And if, before he shut his heavy door, he walked through his rooms to see that all was right, that was simply a natural and rational caution, and did not reflect the infection of terror that seemed to have taken the whole of London in its grip. Or not much.

Sitting room, bedroom, lumber-room. All as they should be. Nobody under the table, nobody under the sofa; a small log burning in the grate. Nobody under the bed; nobody in the closet; nobody in his dressing-gown, which was hanging up like a limp suicide against the wall. Old fire-guard, old shoes, two fish-baskets, washing-stand on three legs, and a poker.

This last item gave Scrooge a weird tingle, as though – in the grisly yet inexplicably popular adage – somebody were walking over his grave. Hadn't the insane fellow at the bridge said something about the poker? But that had been nonsense, and assuredly mad nonsense, and probably *drunk* mad nonsense, and above all *safe-to-ignore* drunk mad nonsense. Scrooge had no need of any poker.

He closed his door, and locked himself in; double-locked himself in. Thus secured against surprise, he took off his day-clothes, put on his nightgown, dressing gown and bedsocks, fixed his nightcap upon his head; and sat down before the fire to warm himself after his chilly walk home.

Outside, the church clock chimed its mournful chime.

It was a very low fire indeed, barely anything against so bitter a night. He was obliged to sit close to it, and brood over it, before he could extract the least sensation of warmth from such a small log. Although the night through which he had just walked had been windless, a mournful winter breeze appeared to have started up in the court, and to be practising its vowels, beginning with the 'o's. Scrooge listened to the *oo* and then again to the *oooo*. There was a crunch to the sound that was unwindlike; and that gave the wail an unpleasant resemblance to his own name. 'Scrooooo ...' it seemed to say.

It was growing in volume. It almost sounded as though it were coming up the stairs inside the building. 'Scroo-oo-oo-ooge ...'

As if the wind could talk! 'I've have always found the pathetic fallacy,' said Scrooge aloud, to himself, to shore up his spirits, 'a pathetic notion.' He listened again, and it did sound as if some unearthly force were calling his name.

'Nonsense,' said Scrooge.

But it was not nonsense. It was indeed, non-nonsense. It was, I mean to say, the opposite of nonsense, in that it was deadly serious. Unnonsense. It was *sense*, is what I – that,

I think, is what I'm trying to say there, with the whole 'not nonsense' thing. Got a bit tangled up, but you see what I mean.

The sensical nature of this threat became unignorable with a deafening crash at Scrooge's door – right there, just outside his apartment! Scrooge jolted with a mighty jolt – he could not be blamed for that; any man would jolt under such circumstances. He jolted himself into a standing position with the shock of the noise.

'Who's there?' he called out.

'Scroo-ooo-oooge ...' replied the visitor. Then he tried his voice at a different vowel: 'Braaaiiins!'

'Brains?' snapped Scrooge. 'Go away, sir, whoever you may be. If you are a carol singer then your rendition deserves no monetary recompense, for it is neither tuneful nor seasonal. If you come to threaten me, then you should know that my door is double-locked, and cannot be breached.'

At that, as if responding to a taunt, there was another mighty thump, and the door shook in its frame. Again a mighty blow was landed upon the door from outside.

Scrooge was startled by the vehemence of this battery; but he was not an individual to be unmanned by fear. I believe I have already mentioned his *froid*, and that it would best be described as *sang*. Or, you know, vice versa. At any rate, he kept a small pistol, armed and primed, on a ledge directly above the door; and he kept it for just such an occasion as this. Accordingly, as the door shook under the repeated blows from outside, he bethought himself not only to retrieve this weapon but also to warn his would-be assailant of its existence.

'Is it you, from the bridge, sirrah?' he shouted at the blank face of his front door, reaching up and bringing down the pistol. 'You who bellowed my name out there, and wittered that gibberish about putting a gold *bar* in my drawers? Well I have in my hand, sir, a loaded pistol. I am quite ready to discharge it, and with pleasure too, into your heart.'

'Scroo-ooo-ooge!'

Crash, bash, smash.

'You'll not breach this door, sir,' said Scrooge without conviction, stepping back involuntarily as each blow landed, and holding the firearm at arm's length before him.

The wood of his door split with a great wrenching sound, and a bloodied fist thrust through the gap. Two boards fell aside, and Scrooge cried out in sudden fear.

The fist withdrew, and was replaced by a face – a hideous, distorted face with dried gore smeared in amongst its whiskers, and yet a face that Scrooge recognised at once. And the slavering mouth expanded its vowel-repertoire: 'Hee-ere's *Marley*!'

Scrooge gulped, and aimed his gun; but his hand was trembling, and by the time he had steadied it with his other hand the face had disappeared.

Then the whole door unpacked into chunks and splinters as Marley's burly form crashed through. Scrooge let fly a yelp, a doggy sound. He pulled the trigger. The pistol made an ear-dinning noise, yanked Scrooge's shoulder back in its socket and threw out a hatful of smoke. The bullet hit its target – colliding with Marley's chest at no more range than a yard. Scrooge saw the cloth of Marley's shirt rip, and saw the flesh open and splash blood. He heard the crack as ribs snapped. For an instant he rejoiced to have struck his target at first attempt. But the rejoicing was straightways stifled, for it was instantly evident that this terrible wound incommoded Marley not at all. He did not seem, even, to notice the hole in his chest, and the blood that flowed from it was watery and scarce. He reached forward with both arms, and started towards his former partner, groaning as he came: 'Scroo-oo-ooge!'

Scrooge took a backward steps, his leg trembling. 'Marley?' he cried. 'I don't believe it! I *won't* believe it! I can't believe it!'

'Brains!' said Marley.

Scrooge took a further backward step.

Marley advanced. There was no mistaking him for a live man; if the wounds it carried blithely about its corpus – from the hole in its chest to the skin flapping off in patches revealing raw meat within, and its ruined face – did not say Death clearly enough, then the expression in its unblinking eyes could not be mistaken.

Scrooge took another backward step. His heel went into the bowl of gruel upon the floor, and, as he shifted his weight, and as he was not looking behind himself, the bowl slid. His long legs spread, and a wail leapt from his mouth. He fell acrobatically backwards, dropping the empty pistol – it clattered uselessly against the wall – and landing painfully upon his back.

'Scroo-ooge!'

'Oo-oo-ooh!' echoed Scrooge in a state of sudden and profound terror. He twisted himself onto his front and got onto all fours, preparatory to regaining his feet, turning thus his back upon the monstrous being. But its shuffling advance could still be heard, and as he began to rise Scrooge lifted his face to see, reflected in his free-standing full-length mirror, the creature almost upon him. The ghastly face lurched forward, and Scrooge felt the grasp of stronger-than-human hands upon his hips.

'Aaah!' he screeched, as the grip of the monster drew his pelvis in against its shuddering body. In the mirror he saw Marley's mouth gaping, the yellow snaggle-teeth each set awry in the black gums, as he readied himself to bite hard upon the back of Scrooge's skull. Again it wailed, *'Brains'*. Could it truly be about to feed upon Scrooge's own brain?

Struggle as he might, Scrooge could not release his hips from the beast's grip. It was, quite apart from the danger, and the terror, undignified. 'Nathan,' Scrooge wailed. 'My old partner – my old friend—'

The jaws snapped shut, and with a twist of his head, like a lion at the neck of an antelope, this bestial revenant wrenched a great chunk from the back of Scrooge's head. The chunk consisted of a cotton nightcap, and a great quantity of hair, but the pulling out of this latter brought a yell of pain to Scrooge's mouth. He struggled in the creature's grip, heaving forward, but the only effect of this was that he cracked his forehead against the planks of his floor.

The monstrous Marley, attempting to bite into tasty brains and instead having munched cloth stuffed with hair – such as might delight a sofa-eater, but not calculated to give culinary satisfaction to a devourer of human flesh – spat and roared. He lunged forward for a second bite at exactly the moment that Scrooge's pained skull, bouncing from the wooden floor, reared up backwards. The two heads, one dead, one still living, met with a fierce crack.

The bones in Marley's nose shattered like an eggshell under the impact of a spoon. The force of the impact knocked his head back. But if this caused the creature pain, or even triggered the distant memory of pain somewhere in its being, it made no sign. Instead it tightened its grip upon Scrooge's haunches, and a terrible moan escaped its mouth.

Scrooge certainly felt the pain, as the dead man's nails bit into his flanks. Almost instinctually he kicked out with his legs, the agony giving unusual force to his muscles. A grasshopper would have been proud of the leverage Scrooge achieved under these atypical circumstances, for he rose upright, standing on his two feet, with Marley's cold, vigorous body still upon his back. 'You'll not,' he gasped, with new determination, 'hug—' and he began to lean backwards '—my—' and he tucked his right foot backwards and started staggering backwards, loaded down, '—bum—'

He covered the five yards across the room without having any means of navigating, or even seeing, where he was going. By the time he collided, backwards, with the chest of drawers on the far side he had picked up a surprising amount of speed. The large wooden handle of the top draw was driven between Marley's shoulder-blades and into his spine – or, more precisely, the creature's spine was driven hard *onto* the wooden handle. Scrooge heard the loud snap – a crack, Hell's pop – of the monster's spine being crushed against the teak semi-circle. The suddenness of the impact had knocked the breath out of Scrooge. Its effect upon the Marley-monster was to

force a reflexive muscular spasm into its muscles. The creature's grip released and its arms flung wide, Scrooge toppled forward, freed from the beast.

He scrabbled across the floor, raised himself panting and turned to face his adversary. 'Your spine snapped?' he gasped gloatingly. 'Your back *broken*?'

'Brains!' moaned the beast, its arms flung wide as if in greeting. It writhed, slowly, jerkily, upon its wooden-knob impalement. Of its impaling. Its impaleness. Of its Impellor.

Of its *being impaled*. Yes, I think that's the right one.

'Marley,' said Scrooge, rubbing his forehead where it hurt the most and attempting the challenging task of making sense out of all that had so violently happened. On reflection, though, perhaps 'impaling' was best, after all. 'Why,' Scrooge demanded, 'why attack *me*?'

'Braains!'

'Do you take me for an ass, sir?'

'Braaaay . . .'

'So you do! I'll not heehaw like a donkey for you! You were supposed to be at death's door, sir!'

'Nnnnn . . .'

'Don't deny it. The whole town was talking about it – the last hours of my old colleague, Nathan Marley!'

'Sss . . .' Marley's slow writhing upon the point of the drawer handle was generating a horrible series of clicking and bone-snapping noises. With a twist, and the sound of something clicking very audibly, Marley's arms lowered themselves to his side.

'Why *attack*, me Nathan?' asked Scrooge, feeling round to the back of his head where a good quantity of hair had been pulled out. 'What would make you break down my door – why so desperate to get at *me*?'

It was impossible to read the expression in the entity's eyes.

Another wrench, and another series of snapping sounds, and it lifted its head. 'Scroooge,' it boomed.

'Your back is quite broken, sir,' said Scrooge. 'Not even the evil power you serve can help you in such a case—'

But as he spoke these words Marley took a step forward. And then another step. The semi-circular wooden hand-pull was still embedded in his spine – hooked, as it happened, over the little spur of bone of the eleventh vertebra. But this injury did not seem to incommode the creature's capacity for coordinating bodily motion. As he stepped forward the drawer was pulled out behind it, and by the third step had been pulled entirely free. Then Marley started walking across the floor leaning forward at a pronounced angle, much as a man may make slow progress into a very powerful headwind – counterweighted by the drawer fixed to its back.

The drawer was mostly filled with clothes: spare sets of leggings, waistcoats, and drawers. Drawers that you might wear, I mean. He didn't keep miniature furniture drawers inside his chest of drawers. That would be odd.

'Scrrooooge!' said the monster, his vigour and determination undimmed.

Scrooge looked about the room for a weapon, but his was a sparsely furnished space. There was his pistol, lying on the floor! But he would barely have time to retrieve that, and would surely not be able to reload it. Besides, the hole from his earlier shot was still gaping in Marley's chest, where his heart should be. If one shot had not slowed him down, why should another?

The creature was almost upon him. He darted to the left. The memory of the man at the bridge returned to him: 'Beware Nathan Marley!' the fellow had said. How had he known? What else had that stranger – stranger than most strangers – said? Stuffing gold into furniture, was it? But also 'pick up a poker'. Scrooge gasped. That was better advice.

The creature was standing between him and the fire, but the wooden drawer, and its cargo of clothing, literally fixed into its back, was slowing it down. Scrooge dodged right, cut-in left, and got to the fireplace. The poker, when he hefted it, seemed too small to do much damage. But it was assuredly better than nothing.

'I'll bash your head in, sir!' he yelled, trying to give himself heart. 'Have at you!'

Marley lumbered towards him, relentless as ever, lumbered as he was with a sizeable piece of timber lodged in his lumbar. 'Scroogebrains!' he cried.

'No sir! *Marley's* brains, sir!' Scrooge, courage perking in his veins, took two steps forward and swung the poker, catching Marley on the side of the head. Impact made a solid noise but left no dent or manifest injury. The creature glowered. Scrooge took one step backwards, grasped the handle of the poker with both hands and swung a second time. The blow caromed from Marley's temples, but Scrooge had delivered it with such force that he lost his grip, and the poker bounced backwards into the open fireplace.

Like a metal arrow it buried its tip into the burning log.

Thus disarmed, Scrooge was forced to duck and scramble to the side as Marley lunged. 'Brains!' the monster demanded. Scrooge rushed to the window, and then, as Marley turned to pursue him, ran to the left. His mind was filled with a single thought: retrieve the poker – the only weapon he had – from the fire. He made a feint for the fireplace, but the creature was in the way, and he had to withdraw. He tried again, but again couldn't get past. Finally, with an elaborate series of lurches, finished with a dash, he got back to the fireplace, and took hold of the poker handle.

He pulled hard, like young Arthur with Excalibur; but

instead of being drawn smoothly from its setting, the poker brought the whole log with it. Worse, the metal of the shaft had been heated in the fire. It was, in short, much too hot for Scrooge to hold on to it. He shouted in pain as he span about, and could not help but let go of the handle. The poker, and its attached chunk of wood, flew directly at Marley. The flaming log struck the monster's shoulder, the poker rotated about, and the whole thing fell into the drawer the creature was carrying at its back.

Scrooge put his scorched palm to his mouth, a sense of imminent doom crashing upon him. What could he do? Nothing could stop this beast. There were several fresh logs piled, ready for use beside the fire, and with his left hand he picked each up in turn and hurled it at his enemy. But they bounced uselessly off the creature's chest.

The stench of burning cloth tickled Scrooge's nostrils. Tufts of dark smoke drifted up behind Marley's shoulders. Still he advanced, inexorably, towards Scrooge.

'Nathan—' Scrooge yelled. 'Harken! Is there no human sympathy left inside you?'

'Braains!'

What else was there? Scrooge scuttled like a dog along the floor and picked up the pistol. Reloading this device was a two-minute operation, but he could think of nothing better, and so he ran behind Marley to get to his strong-box, set on a shelf at chest height.

Flames, now, were flickering upwards from the drawer set into Marley's back; the burning log had lit the clothing inside. The hair upon the back of Marley's head was singeing, and the reek was filling the room. But still he did not stop.

Scrooge scrabbled at his pocket for the key to the strong-box and only then realised that he *had* no pocket, that he had already changed out of his day-clothes and into his nightdress.

The key was in his jacket, which was hanging on the clothes hook by the door.

Marley's claw caught his arm, and Scrooge's heart almost burst with terror – but it was not quite his arm, only the material of his nightdress. Cloth ripped and Scrooge hauled himself away, managed to get to the jacket and fumble out the key. Marley's back was manifestly on fire now, but, rather than scorching, the flesh appeared to be melting, like pink and red wax – a repellent state of affairs that had no effect upon the entity's strength or purpose. Scrooge got back to the strong-box and inserted the key.

Before he could turn the key Marley was on him – crashing into him from the right, sinking its nails into the flesh of Scrooge's shoulder and forcing him along the wall.

What happened next passed with such rapidity that it took Scrooge some moments after the event to piece it all together. There was a moment of purest terror, as Marley's teeth reached for the side of Scrooge's head, the beast's grip tight upon his shoulder, the impossibility of escape clanging noisily in Scrooge's thoughts like a death knell.

Then – a clatter, a smash, and the sound of something wetly dislocating and slithering free.

Then – Marley frozen, forceless, no longer gripping Scrooge, his jaw slack and loose. He slumped to the side, and only the presence of the wall prevented him from toppling over completely.

Scrooge scrabblingly extricated himself, and looked about him. His lungs were heaving.

Marley's monstrous revenant had stopped in mid-throttle (in, we might say, *rott*). Blinkingly Scrooge saw what had happened.

Marley's shove, combined with the fact that, through panic, or embedded miserliness, Scrooge had refused to let go the key, had *pulled* the strong-box from its shelf by main force. This in turn had deposited the great weight of the box into the drawer at the revenant's back. The weight of the iron box and its heavy golden contents, dropped into this sturdy wooden trough, had dragged the whole drawer free from Marley's back. The hook of the handle, having got itself snagged firmly over one of the vertebral links of the creature's backbone, had not given up its hold. Accordingly pulling the drawer free had also entailed pulling the spine clean *out* of Marley's back – and with the spine had come out a goodly portion of Marley's brain, sucked as it were down the plughole gap at the base of the skull, to flop and slop down upon the floor.

Scrooge peered at his former partner in astonishment. For, remarkably, even this injury had not entirely deprived his body of motion or volition. There he stood, old Nathan Marley, moaning weakly: '—roo-oo-oo—'.

But at least he was no longer trying to kill him.

Smoke piled upwards towards the ceiling.

It took long moments for Scrooge's self-possession to reassert itself. Then, thinking of the danger to his property, he fetched his washbowl and doused the fire inside the drawer before it could spread further. Marley still stood, swaying gently, and moaning: but no longer a threat. The removal of the upper portion of his spinal chord had given his body a very strange posture. The head had flopped backwards and was balanced on the shoulders, sunk a little between them, with the blank eyes staring directly at the ceiling. It was a peculiar and monstrous sight. The arms hung slack, and horrible goo dripped from the beast's back: pale orange Marley-water dripping down upon the mess below.

Scrooge tested the handle of the poker gingerly, found it cool enough to hold, and pulled the metal bar from the log and drawer. Then, readying himself, he said: 'I feel almost as if I should apologise, old partner.' But he did not apologise. With half a dozen swift, well-aimed strokes he brought the poker down from above and smashed Marley's head to bloody pieces. The body slumped and crashed onto the floor.

'Tis the season,' Scrooge gasped, exhausted by the effort, yet with a shuddery sort of triumph flaring inside him, 'to thee *bury* . . .'

THE FIRST SPIRIT

Scrooge collapsed, exhausted, upon his bed. He did not sleep – could not so much as close his eyes, in the febrile terror and aftershock of what he had just endured. From time to time he would lift his eyes: there lay the motionless, twice-dead body of Nathan Marley. The candle was burning down, and its flame shaking, which caused the shadows in at Marley's side to swell and shrink, as if struggling to escape being pinned under so nameless a horror.

He was endeavouring, and failing, to tear his eyes from this grisly sight when the chimes of a neighbouring church struck the four quarters. He listened for the hour. The heavy bell tolled once, twice, thrice, and stopped. It was a new day – it was Christmas day. Never had he experienced a Christmas like that.

He was trembling. 'What,' he muttered, 'what a *shock* I have endured.'

He was conscious of the need to pass water – the excitement of the battle with Marley had distracted him from the urgency of this physical need. He was still trembling with the after-effects of his exertions, and his terror, as he sat upright and pulled the chamber pot from under the bed.

It took half a minute to decant the contents of his bladder into the pot; the heat of this fluid, in the cold air of the midnight winter room, generated billows of steam. It poured in folds and clouds, granulated white, and coiled about Scrooge's ankles. When he had finished relieving himself Scrooge sat back and tried to calm his chirruping heart. 'I am too old for such shocks,' he said.

The bowl sat on the floorboards, smoking. Scrooge pondered getting up and going to the window to empty it. Leave it until the morning, he thought, but this thought only reminded him the more forcefully of the presence in his room of the battered and crushed body of That Which Had Once Been Marley. Should he leave that until the morning as well? To sleep in the same room as his former partner's mutilated corpse was too horrible a thought. Yet it was the small hours of Christmas Morning – not yet dawn. How could he even reach the authorities?

He waved his hand to disperse the clouds of steam, but if anything they seemed to be thickening. It was certainly very cold in the room.

The best thing, perhaps, would be to find an inn prepared to admit him where he could sleep and steady himself. It was late, but who would turn away a supplicant on Christmas Morning? Of course, no sooner had he bethought himself of this than the answer presented itself in a piercing inner voice: *You* would, Scrooge. *You* would.

'I am shaken,' he said aloud. 'I am shaken. Sometimes a man falls, incrementally, into bad habits. Sometimes it takes a severe jolt to shake a man *out* of such habits.'

The billows of steam from his filled chamber pot were fuller and broader than ever. That faintly turnipy, slightly tart odour was in Scrooge's nostril. Surprised, he looked around himself and saw the whole bedroom was filled with white steam. 'Do I bathe *a la Turque*?' he expostulated. 'Or is the room on fire after all?'

But, getting up from the bed and searching about, it was clear that the white clouds roiling and coiling about so prodigiously were truly steam, and not smoke. Never, in all his years of using a chamber pot in cold rooms, had Scrooge seen the like. And as he stood rubbing the back of his head, where a bald patch had been so aggressively thinned, the steam began to coil in the same direction.

This, clearly, was a more than natural phenomenon.

The white steam swirled about Scrooge, placing him at the centre – as it were – of a whirlpool of cloud. At first the clouds moved slowly, and he could follow the motion with his eye. Soon, though, they accelerated, and the whole room was blotted in a blurring mist of white. No sooner had this *tourbillon* begun upon its spin than it changed, tightening its vortex and shifting like a miniature hurricane to trace a path about the room. The vapour distilled into this shape, and Scrooge could again see his own walls and furniture – again see the body of Marley laid by the wall – and for a moment he considered rushing to the splintered door and dashing out into the night, dressed in his nightwear as he was.

But, before he could move, the white clouds tightened, shuddered and ceased their motion. Where once there had been only steam, now a being – an entity, or Spirit, or ghost – was standing: palely transparent, two arms and two legs, and a face composed of whiteness, with eyes that took a moment to focus.

The newcomer looked at Scrooge. 'Oh!'

'Oh!' said Scrooge.

'Gracious!' said the apparition.

'Oh!' said Scrooge, again.

'Well, let us not get off on the wrong foot. Good evening. How are you?'

'Oh!' said Scrooge, again. He really couldn't think of a better answer.

'I'm very pleased to meet you,' said the ghost. 'You don't mind if I have a quick look around? I am, by nature, a little on the timid side.'

Scrooge shook his head, to indicate either that he had no objection, or else to express a more general non-comprehension.

The ghost put out a ghostly leg and embarked upon his ghostly going, both toing and froing. It, or he – for now he had fully taken the form of a white-skinned gentleman dressed all in white, although of such transparency that it was possible to see the wall directly through him – examined the broken fixtures and fittings with the assiduity of a landlord calculating the necessary diminution of a tenant's deposit. Finally, he stood before the smashed-in body of Marley. 'Dear me,' he said, with the faintest note of distaste in his voice. 'You chewed this one up and spat him out, didn't you?'

'He,' said Scrooge, still shivery with the aftershock. 'That.'

'A Zombie.'

'A monster! A savage being who sought out my violent death!'

'I know.' The Spirit seemed disproportionately incommoded by the presence of Marley's corpse, and went so far as to retreat to the far side of the room and stand in front of a chromolithographic portrait of the Queen – Her Majesty being perfectly visible through the entity's chest and stomach. 'It is – deactivated?'

'Dead, you mean?' said Scrooge.

'Dead doesn't perhaps mean what you think,' said the ghost. 'Being dead doesn't slow *them* down one jot. I mean *deactivated.*' The Spirit looked so timidly, as if it might flee out of the window at the slightest twitch of the supine corpse, that Scrooge was prompted to ask: 'You are *afraid* of it? Of them?'

'I am absolutely and assuredly afraid of Zombies,' said the ghost. '*They* are fearful things. Quite apart from anything, they are *extremely* difficult to deactivate. If you have managed it, my friend, then I take off my hat to you.' He wasn't wearing a hat, but the ghost did have a white spiritual periwig lying over his scalp, and he swept this off and bowed. 'If you have truly been able to put a stop to this Zombie's predations, then you are indeed the person we are looking for. It is not everybody who can overcome something as relentless as . . .' And the Spirit seemed to shudder from toe to crown as it looked at the remains of Marley. '*It.*'

'*He,*' Scrooge corrected, shivering himself with the thought of what he had done, 'had a name. He was Nathan Marley – my per, my per-partner.' Scrooge coughed 'Bah!'

'I must correct you, dear sir. It may once *have been* Nathan Marleymiper. But it ceased being that person as soon as the Zombie virus infected it.'

'I do not know this term, sir.'

'The word is linked to the Greek "Ζωον" – a living being, an animal – which is to say, "Ζωος" "life, alive". And it derives, also, from βιός, which also means "life". You'll know both these Greek terms, sir, for English words have been derived from them: zoology, biology, the twin studies of living things.'

'Living beings?'

'I assume the logic is that such beings are imbrued with a double life; for when one life was taken away, they lurched back into life again, although life of a different sort. Hence they named them, living beings, the persistence of life: *ƶōon-*

bios.' Again the Spirit shook so profoundly that the pigtail of his spirit-wig jiggled.

Scrooge found his curiosity to be greater even than his shock. 'You tremble with fear, sir?'

'I do.'

'You are a ghost?'

'Indeed,' said the ghost.

'Yet you are yourself terrified?'

'And why should that surprise you?'

'Because,' Scrooge said, 'I had always heard that ghosts were in the business of scaring others, not being scared themselves.'

'If you'll forgive me, sir, that shows how little you know. Do you see that I am transparent?'

'I can hardly avoid seeing it, sir.'

'It is, you'll concede, well known that ghosts are transparent beings?'

'Yes.'

'And have you ever wondered *why* ghosts are transparent?'

'Because,' Scrooge started, but he was compelled to stop and think about this. 'I do not know. Is it to do with your immateriality?'

'Pshaw,' said the Spirit. 'Whilst it is true my kind is ideational, rather than material, that hardly entails transparency. Think of the other ideational beings with which you are familiar: your dreams, the creations of literature and art. Are they transparent?'

'No,' Scrooge conceded.

'Hamlet and Odysseus – are *they* transparent?'

'No.'

'When you recall people to your mind, are they transparent in your memory?'

'No.'

'There you go then.'

'And yet you *are*,' Scrooge pointed out.

'I'm sure you can deduce why *we* – I mean, my kind – are this way.'

Scrooge thought for a moment, but shook his head. 'I suspect my powers of deduction have been too profoundly shaken up by the events of this night.'

'What creatures are transparent in the natural world?' the Spirit prompted.

'I do not know that any are,' returned Scrooge. 'Save, perhaps, jellyfish. Polyps and small fishes of the deep. Some insects, I suppose.'

'And why are they so?'

'I really don't know.'

'*Disguise*,' said the Spirit. 'They hope, in their transparency, to evade the glance of the predator. To take on the colour of air, or water, itself.'

Scrooge furrowed his brow. 'You are saying that ghosts are . . . ?'

'We are timid beings. Why do you think we appear so infrequently? And we have good reason to be timid. Our transparency is camouflage. For there are entities in the world that seek to devour us. *We* the prey, and *they* the predator . . .'

Scrooge, standing by the bed, took the few steps towards Marley's remains.

'Entities such as this?' he asked, tapping Marley's lifeless foot with his own toe. The gesture was enough to send a tremble through the dead flesh; and this motion by itself caused the Spirit to squeal in fear and to hide its face behind its hands. Since its hands were transparent, this was a gesture of limited usefulness.

'Don't! Please don't do that! You have no idea how alarming those creatures are to . . . to the likes of me.'

'But do they truly *eat* you?' asked Scrooge. 'I mean no offence, sir, but I find it hard to imagine that . . . one such as you . . . represent much of a *meal*.'

'Understand this about Zombies. They feed upon *mind*. They devour mentition itself. If they come upon you then they will break open your skull and slurp up your brains. With me, should they chance upon me, and because I am wholly ideational, they would devour me entire. And very unpleasant it would be.' Once again the Spirit shuddered.

'It would . . . kill you?' Scrooge asked.

'Indeed!'

'But, you are a ghost. Are you not *already* dead?'

At this the Spirit laughed, a tinkly, chiming, bell-like sound. 'What queer ideas you have about Spirits, Ebeneezer! You don't mind if I call you Ebeneezer?'

'You know what?' Scrooge asked, looking about the ruin of his apartment. 'If all this did not seem so very . . . vivid . . . then I would say it is all a very bad dream. I would like *very much* to believe it is a dream. Perhaps you, Spirit, who know of these things – for did you not mention the dreaming world as ideational and akin to yours – can reassure me on that score? Will I wake, soon, to an ordinary world?'

'This is no dream, Ebeneezer,' said the Spirit, gravely.

'If you are not the ghost of a dead person,' Scrooge asked. 'Then what *are* you?'

'I'm glad you asked me that,' said the Spirit.

'There are three of us – three brothers, if you like,' said the Spirit. 'Past, Present and Future.'

'Three Spirits?'

'Indeed. And we have been scheduled to visit you. I have

the honour of being the first. How do you do?' He bowed. 'In fact, we have travelled a long way to – reach you,' said the Spirit.

'And which one are you – the Past?' Scrooge asked.

But the Spirit shook its head. 'The Past is dead,' he said; which either meant he was talking about the individual decease of his brother, or else offering a general as-it-were philosophic observation about the whole of history.

'My, er, commiserations,' said Scrooge, uncertainly.

'The past is necessarily dead,' said the Spirit. 'Life is volition and change and potential. The past has none of that. It is a child's observation to say as much. But the present is alive, and the present holds hands with the future – will, change, potential.'

'So you are the Present.'

'I am: Christmas Present.'

'I would have thought Past, Present and Future would have been a more logical progression.'

'You would have thought that,' said the Spirit. 'But only because you haven't thought about it properly.'

'But why *Christmas*?'

'There are reasons, and they are important reasons,' said the ghost. 'But one thing at a time. Explanation-wise, I mean.'

'Spirit – forgive me – are you saying that your brother Spirit, who bears the name Past, is himself dead? Or do you merely mean that things, once they have happened, pass into the afterlife?'

'Merely?' chuckled the Spirit. 'There's a cosmos tangled up in your word, *merely*, there. My brother can move and speak.'

'Then he's alive.'

'Not everything that can move and speak is alive,' the Spirit of the Present noted, gesturing theatrically to Marley's supine corpse.

'But can a *Spirit* truly be Zombified?'

'If it can happen to flesh, then why not to Spirit? If flesh can be born, live, grown, then so can Spirit. If flesh can weaken, sicken, feel pain and die, then so can Spirit. And if the Spirit can die, why can it not return from death in Zombie form?'

Scrooge shuddered, looking at the figure spread before him.

'You spoke,' he said, shortly, 'of life as being volition, change and potential. Do Zombies possess none of these qualities?'

'None,' said the Spirit. 'Their will is dead. In its place is only a linear, implacable urge to feed on the flesh of the living. They cannot change; cannot learn, or grow, or alter. Nor do they embody potential. Theirs is the opposite of potential: entropy is the word to describe them.'

From outside in the yard there came, as if on cue, a mighty wail. 'Scroo-oo-ooge!'

The Spirit darted to the window. 'Talk of the Devil,' he said.

'The Devil is a creature of theological conjecture and folk belief,' Scrooge began, 'the embodiment of ultimate evil and generally thought of as in implacable opposition to the primary principle of Good—'

'No,' said the ghost. 'What I mean is: just as I was explaining to you the nature of Zombies, so a clutch of Zombies comes into the yard below your apartment.'

Scrooge hurried to the window. It was true: down below, lit by the paling light of imminent dawn, half a dozen lurching bodies were converging on the entrance to his building. Some had their arms straight out in front of them. One, blood congealed in a black cowl all over his face, carried the severed head of some poor fellow swinging in the grip of its left hand like a trophy.

'There are more of them?'

'Now that it is Christmas Day,' said the Spirit, 'I'm afraid a great many have awoken. And these ones have come specifically for you, Ebeneezer.'

'But why me?' Scrooge demanded.

'I daresay,' the ghost went on, in a slightly trembling voice, 'that the door to this building is solid oak, well locked and secured against intrusion. It will not hold them for ever, for they will batter and beat upon it for as long as it takes to break it down. But it will hold them for some time.'

'The main entrance to the building,' said Scrooge, 'is unlocked and, I believe, open.'

The ghost looked at him with his semi-transparent, white eyes. 'Very well,' he said, shortly. 'But at least the door to your apartment is . . .' As he spoke he turned to look at the main door, hanging in shreds and splinters from a smashed frame. 'Your door is in a state of considerable disrepair,' he noted.

'I'm afraid so.'

'It does not matter,' said the ghost. From below, the sounds of multiple Zombies moaning 'Scrooge!' and 'Scroo-ooge!' was growing louder. 'But of course there is a back exit, a way of sneaking out of the building that avoids the main stairwell?'

'There is no such exit,' said Scrooge. 'The only way out is through the front door and across the yard down there.' He gestured down: a dozen or more Zombies had come into the yard.

'Very well,' said the ghost again, his voice tight. 'You understand that these monsters are *coming* for you?'

'I don't understand! I mean – I understand *that* they are,

but not *why*. Why me?' repeated Scrooge, wide-eyed. 'What animus do they have against *me*, individually?'

'They recognise, on the level of their minds capable of recognising anything at all, that you are a great threat to their kind.'

'I?' boggled Scrooge.

'More precisely, they have been sent – in effect – by the malign entity that spread this plague – here, in London town, in this era. *He* knows you are a threat, and Zombies are his tool. They are coming for you, but will devour me at the same time. They will snap me up as a kingfisher does a stickleback. Do you understand?'

'And what will they do to me?'

'They will devour your brains, of course. But me – because I am pure mentition – they will eat the whole of me. I am in a worse position than you.'

'*Nobody* is in a worse position than I!' Scrooge broke out. 'On Christmas Eve I was a respected trader on the Exchange. It is not yet Christmas Morning, and now I am hunted by a pack of brain-eating Jumblies.'

'Zombies,' corrected the ghost.

'Zoom Bees.'

'Zom. Zom. It's a short "o". Try it.'

'Zom.'

'That's it.'

'Zomzoms.'

'Just one zom.'

Scrooge looked anxiously at the window. 'Zoms?'

'Good! Now add the *bee* . . .'

'Look, could we perhaps have this conversation some other time? Only I'm quite keen to get away . . .'

'Won't take a moment,' said the Spirit. 'Just like to hear you say it right . . .'

'Zer-zom? Sorry, sorry. Zomzoms.'

'Like I said, just *one* zom: zombies. Repeat—'

'Zombies,' said Scrooge.

'Excellent!'

Scrooge put his hands to his face. 'Oh it's hopeless!'

'No, that was a pretty good pronunciation.'

'I don't mean that. I mean – escape. Hopeless! Ghost, shall I tell you something? I was a happy child. I had friends – I had prospects. Then something happened to me – an attack, unprovoked and most distressing, not unlike what is happening here. Since then, and for decades now, I have been the loneliest, most unhappy individual in this entire city! People call me a miser, make jokes behind my back. Nobody comprehends my loneliness! My melancholy! And now, in addition to those years of suffering . . . now this?'

The sound of Zombie feet was only too audible coming up the main staircase outside.

'Tush!' said the Spirit. 'How can you *say* you are lonely? Let me take you by the hand, Scrooge, and show you all the streets of London, Scrooge. I will show you something that will make you change your Scrooge. Your mind, rather.'

The Spirit laid his hand in ghostly fingers – it felt like a breeze upon the skin, or a strange tingle, but Scrooge could sense the presence of the entity – and began to lift up in the air. 'You are flying, sir!' Scrooge said.

'I am.'

Scrooge felt his stomach yawn. His toes drooped. The whole room seemed to shift about him. '*I* am flying, sir!'

'You are.'

'How? I mean, by what means . . . ?'

'So long as I have hold of you,' said the Spirit, 'I can elevate you.'

'Why don't we fall?'

'Technically speaking we *are* falling. The whole world is falling all the time. I'm just reorienting us both a little with respect to that. Think of it as falling with greater *style*. Come! Come, and I shall show you London this very night!' The Spirit of the Present stretched out his free arm. 'To inner Finsbury,' he cried. 'And *beyond*!'

With a whoosh they swept through the room straight at the far wall. The Spirit passed through the brickwork like water through a grill – he soared onward into the night sky. Scrooge, however, possessed considerably less interpenetrability. He struck the plasterboard with a smack loud enough to make the pictures on their hooks shake and jiggle. He possessed enough forward momentum to flatten his whole body hard against the wall, arms and legs akimbo. For a moment – the precise length of time determined according to the laws of the physics of comic potentialisation – Scrooge hung, spread-eagled, upon the vertical surface. Then, with a squeaky sound, he slid downwards. His feet snagged on the skirting board and he tumbled backwards onto the floor, landing with a thud. He uttered a single word. To be precise it was not so much a word as a syllable, although it was an expressive and semantically efficient syllable. 'Ow,' he said.

The Spirit of Christmas Present reappeared through the wall. 'Sorry!' he chirruped. 'Forgetful of me. I apologise.'

Something of Scrooge's habitual grumpiness – a quality that had been dissolved by the extraordinary events of the evening – re-emerged. He sat up, rubbing his nose. 'What the bloody Hell,' he enquired, 'do you think you are *playing at*?'

'Let's open the window,' said the Spirit, 'and have another go at that.'

London was spread out below them under the thinning dark of the pre-dawn. Though it was cold, and dark, there were many revellers out enjoying themselves. The two of them swooped down low upon a splotch of light, which revealed itself to be a public house. Drinkers spilled through the bright-lit door onto the pavement, mugs of foaming ale in their hands. Or, to be more precise, the *mugs* in their hands, the ale in their bellies and the foam in their beards and down their tunics.

Scrooge and the Spirit touched down in the shadows, not far from the open entrance, where drinkers milled about. 'Another!' bellowed one of these, a man with a huge beard the colour of shag-tobacco. 'My round! What you having?'

'Beer,' cried the man to his left.

'Beer,' said a second, swaying man.

'Bleurch,' said a third, who was vomiting into the gutter.

'What's that?' said the black-bearded man. 'Didn't quite catch that.'

'I said,' repeated the man, on all fours, '*beer*.'

'Right! Right! Beer. Anybody else? What about you lot?'

'Beer!'

'Beer!'

'Beer!'

'Braains!'

'So let's have a quick tally,' said the black-bearded fellow. 'That's *six* beers and *one* – wa-a-ait a sec. What was that last one again?'

Instead of answering this question with words, the new-comer lunged forward and grabbed the bearded man's ears with his hand. 'Oi!' quickly became, 'Ow!' which in turn rapidly became a scream loud enough to stop all the chatter outside and inside the pub. The drinkers, their wits befuddled with Yuletide drinking, made at first no move to separate the two. It looked, incongruously enough, as if the two men were kissing. The bearded fellow struggled, feebly at first, but then as the agony intensified to the point where it overwhelmed the analgesic sluggishness of the alcohol in the man's bloodstream, with a desperate, writhing, horrible vigour. But although his legs thrashed and his heels clattered on the paving-stones, he could not break free from the Zombie's grip.

'The Zombies prefer,' said the Spirit in a low tone, directly into Scrooge's ear, 'to go in at the front.'

'The face!' shuddered Scrooge. 'But why?'

'It is brains they want, and the human skull is thicker at the back and sides. The front is more accessible – through the thinner bones of the cheeks, the holes of eye-socket and nose. You see.'

The men, stunned as much by drink as by what they were seeing, were beginning to rouse themselves. 'Hey!' 'What's your game?' 'Oi, leave him be!'

The bearded man's screams were becoming spluttery gurgles now. His right ear had become detached, and the Zombie had discarded this only to clamp his hand back onto the side of his head. One drinker put a hand on the creature's shoulder. The bearded man's legs stopped twitching and dangled motionless. Over the noise of outraged men the horrible slurping, chomping sound was audible.

'Must we watch this disgusting display?' asked Scrooge, genuinely distressed. His chilly miser's heart, which found it easy to ignore low-level human misery, was jolted by this encounter with more acute suffering. He had, after all, narrowly escaped a similar fate only a few hours earlier in his own apartment. He felt the stirrings of common humanity at the fate of this blameless Christmas toper.

'I must show you the terrible events of the day,' said the

Spirit, in a low voice. 'You must understand. With the dawn of the day – Christmas Day – this plague will spread rapidly though the entire city. By nightfall the population will be divided into those infected and turned into Zombies, and those desperate to get away.'

The Zombie had dropped his first victim to the floor, and was turning towards a second.

'Some of these mortals will die here, their brains consumed,' the Spirit explained. 'Others will flee, but will carry the plague inside them. It takes the form of – let us say, of an animalcule inside the blood. Once it is inside your body, and depending upon various factors, you will take a few minutes, or hours, or in some cases days, to be transformed.'

Scrooge shuddered. 'Spirit,' he said, 'have *I* been so infected? By my encounter with Marley?'

'No, Scrooge. Of all humanity you alone are immune to the plague.'

'I? Why I?'

'Did you,' the ghost said, turning to face Scrooge, 'say *wye-aye!*'

'No. I asked why I, alone amongst all of humanity, should be immune.'

'Oh, good. I was going to say; I'm not sure the occasion merits a celebratory utterance like *wye-aye.*'

The Zombie was shaking the hand of one of the drinkers. This phrase, in conventional use, would suggest that he was grasping the other man's hand lightly but firmly and imparting an up-down motion to it, such that the arm pivots easily on the shoulder joint. But the Zombie was not shaking the drinker's hand in that sense. Rather he had, in point of fact, wholly removed the man's hand from its arm, and was flapping the severed organ above his head, roaring, 'Coo-ooo-ee!'

The Spirit, clearly made nervous by his proximity to the

creature, took hold of Scrooge's wrist, and together the two lifted up into the sky. 'But what is it *doing*?' Scrooge asked. 'Is it mad?'

'Devouring the drunk man's brains has intoxicated it.'

The Zombie now appeared to be assisting the vomiting man by reaching down his throat and hauling up the whole stomach – and its nauseous contents – in one go. Men were starting to run away. The fellow whose hand had been torn off was on his knees, screaming, watching his lifeblood gush from the stump like water from a fireman's hose.

The Spirit lifted Scrooge away. 'Thank Heavens you have removed me, Spirit! What horrors!'

'There are other horrors to see,' said the ghost, grimly.

They passed over Covent Garden, where Christmas traders were readying their stalls in the pre-dawn: turkeys and winter vegetables. Scrooge and the ghost swooped low over this scene, invisible to the men and women, but able to see them and to hear their merry banter. They were unloading stock from a number of carts and readying it on their stalls by the light of a number of lanterns hanging from the awnings.

Scrooge saw a poulterer carrying two huge turkeys — recently killed and as yet unplucked — from his cart over to his stall. 'These two are prize winners,' he called to his colleagues. 'Biggest of the flock! A guinea each!'

'They were sickening, ready to pop their clogs!' returned another trader. 'I saw them on the cart. You've got rotten poultry, there.'

'Nothing the customers need to know. I've wrung their necks now,' said the first. But as far as this went he did not appear to have done a very good job; for as he plonked them down on the boards of his stall they twitched, sat up and looked about.

The trader had his back to the stall, fetching more stock from his cart. When he turned around, two more birds in his hand he expressed surprise. 'Aye-aye, chips and pie!' he ejaculated. 'What's *this*?'

The second trader moseyed over to the cart. 'Wrung their necks, you said? Losing your touch, are you, George?'

'I'll ring 'em now,' said George, crossly, plonking two new birds on the stall to free up his hands. 'Ring 'em harder than Saint Clements.'

The two turkeys looked at one another. 'Gobble?' said one to the other.

'Gobble?' said the other to the one.

Scrooge had the uncanny feeling that this exchange constituted an actual communication between the two.

As George lifted the two birds, one in each hand, ready to throttle them a second time, they acted in unison. Flapping their wings furiously and flurrying forwards, each beak found an eye. George screamed, let go his grip and instead tried to use his hands to bat the creatures away. But they beat their wings furiously and paddled their feet upon the man's chest, and in a twinkling they had each pecked out a jellied eyeball. They were not interested in the eyes, of course. Instead they thrust their heads hard into the sockets and began to gobble in earnest.

George's screaming assumed a wineglass-shattering pitch. The second trader took the Lord's name in vain several times, stumbling backwards in horror.

The turkeys had sunk their heads and necks into the eye-sockets of George's skull – thrust themselves in up to the hilt. The poor man ran, bellowing, blindly, his arms out, the two monstrously wriggling bodies of the birds fixed firmly to his face.

Scrooge looked away. The commotion was spreading through the market now – other animals, slain for the Christmas table, were reanimating. And at the edge of the square, to the south, Zombies in human form were stumbling and moaning into the crowd. Shrieks rent the air. Indeed, it would be better to say that shrieks possessed the air freehold; for there was no sense of temporary ownership about these songs of human misery.

Scrooge felt the wind intensify, and his legs hang slack. He looked again, and saw that he was once again airborne, with the Spirit's hand upon his forearm. Covent Garden was sinking away below him. 'This plague,' he stuttered. 'It can infect animals as well as humans?'

'What are humans except advanced animals?' returned the Spirit, gloomily. 'But the – animalcule, the tiny zöo-microbot, that causes the condition – it *prefers* humans.'

'Why?'

'Because it feeds upon mind, and the harvest of thought is thin amongst animals – non-existent amongst many. Mankind provides it with the richest harvest. Generally speaking, if it infects animals it only does so in order to get at people.'

'You make it sound like this disease is itself conscious!'

'It *is* clever,' said the ghost. 'Not conscious, exactly, but . . . canny.'

'Oh, what hope is there?' wailed Scrooge, in a despairing voice.

'There is you,' said the ghost. He turned in the air, like a glider, and took Scrooge eastward.

They flew over Whitechapel, a poorer part of the city. Here too, though, the inhabitants were readying themselves for Christmas Morning. Some windows showed the faint gleam of lit candles. On a normal day, at this hour, workmen and workwomen would be stepping, yawning, through doorways – but on this one day, of all the year, work was forgotten.

Yet most is not all. For here, as they swept lower, Scrooge made out one man, better dressed than you might expect to find in Whitechapel, scurrying along the road. He was wearing a black frock coat and hat, and carrying a little black bag. A doctor, Scrooge bethought himself. The hurrying figure ducked into an alley, and came to a halt in front of a young woman standing at the corner. From her apparel – the nature of her patched threadbare dress, the amount of leg she displayed – quite as much as the fact of her waiting at a street corner in this manner, it was clear enough what her occupation was. The ghost brought Scrooge down to the roof of a single-storey building on the other side of the alley, and they peered over the eaves to watch what unfolded.

The man was standing in a pool of light cast from a street lamp, but the woman stood in the shadows.

'Hello my dear,' said the black-clad stranger, in an unctuous and unpleasant voice. It sounded, to Scrooge's ears, oddly familiar – well-spoken and distinctive – although he couldn't quite place from where he recognised it.

The woman muttered something. It was certainly cold enough, and she was scantily dressed enough, to explain the 'brr' that emerged from her lips.

'And what would you charge me, m'dear?' enquired the man, hugging his little black bag to his chest with what looked to Scrooge almost like glee.

The woman uttered an indistinct syllable.

'What was that? Eight? Did you say eight?'

'... eeiiigh ...'

'That's pricey, m'dear!'

'Ssss ...'

'Shillings? Too *much* lucre! I'll tell you what, m'dear.' He snapped open his bag, and Scrooge caught sight of something gleaming inside. 'I shall have to be quick,' he said. 'There's a lot to get through, what with the necessary Masonic, kabbalistic, Satanist, voodoo, Anglican, Women's Institute and International Rules of Cricket *rituals* that I must perform – for reasons I don't have time to go into right now. But it's not something *you* need worry about, my dear woman. It won't take me more than ten minutes to ...' And from the bag he brought out, with a flourish, a surgical scalpel. 'To fillet you like a *kipper*!'

His arm darted out with a practised motion: the scalpel intersected the woman's throat and came back into the light dark with blood.

'Ha-ha!' crowed the man. 'Behold, I am no ordinary man!' The woman lurched forward, the sounds from her mouth becoming more, rather than less, distinct. 'Braains!'

'Yes! Look upon your doom!' the man was saying. 'For I am *Jack* – Jack the . . .' The woman's face loomed forward into the light, and the fellow's voice shifted abruptly in tone, from gloat to shriek '. . . r-r-RUDDY *NORA*!'

The streetwalker's face was caked in dried blood, her mouth wide in a terrifying grimace. The blood that dribbled from the cut in her neck was watery and thin.

Jack heaved his bag upwards with all his might, crying 'eeek!' at piercing volume. The blow clunked the woman's chin and knocked her head back, stretching the gash in her neck. She pawed the air, almost got hold of his coat lapels, missing only by a fraction. Jack, dropping his bag, danced backwards. 'HELP!' he yelled. 'Police! Help, ho! Somebody, for the love of all that's holy!'

He turned to run, and collided almost immediately with a second Lady of the Night, who was just at that moment coming up the alley. He bounced off her frontage, and sat down hard upon the cobblestones. Still shrieking for help, he span about on his rear, pitched forward into a sprinter's starting position and tried to launch forward into a hundred yard dash, and freedom. But the second woman's arm had darted forward, between Jack's legs, and her hand had evidently lighted upon some point of purchase in there. Her grip was firm enough that, though the man put all the muscular strength of his legs into launching off, all he succeeded in doing was tipping himself over and cracking his forehead upon the cobbles. Not releasing her grip, and displaying astonishing strength, this second woman raised her arm, and Jack was quickly suspended upside-down in mid-air. He was no longer shouting 'Help!' or 'Police!' The shouts were now more along the lines of 'nooo!' and 'aaargh!'

The strength in the second woman's grip was truly pro-digious. She angled her arm higher, and Jack's head came up to chest height. Blood was dribbling down his forehead where it had struck the road. His cries of fear and pain were terrible to hear.

The first woman approached. 'Braains,' she uttered, leaning forward a little.

'Please!' begged Jack shriekingly. 'Please, spare me! Oh, the *pain*!'

His hat fell off.

The woman put out both her hands and ran fingers over Jack's forehead. It looked almost as though she was acting with tenderness, exploring his wound with a view to tending it; and Scrooge – watching it all – felt a flush of hope. Perhaps this woman, however degraded she might be now, had once been a nurse, or some sister of mercy? Perhaps, despite the awful ravages of this Zombie plague, she was experiencing some flash-back of pity for her victim? Could it be that the wound had stirred some still-human portion of her con-sciousness? Could it be that she was warmed by some spark of retained humanity?

The answer to all these questions, it quickly transpired was: no.

She found the point of the wound, where the skin had been broken and a small chip knocked from the skull. Into this she worked first the forefinger of her right, and then the forefinger of her left, hand. As Jack's screams intensified, and his flailing arms flew wilder, she poked through, widening the hole. Soon enough, and whilst the dangling man emptied howl upon howl from his lungs, she was able to fit three fingers on either side. Then, with a forceful motion, like a diner in a fish restaurant opening a lobster, she yanked the skull sim-ultaneously left and right, splitting it wide. The contents sagged free with a revolting sound. Both women grabbed handfuls and thrust it into their mouths.

*

The ghost took Scrooge high into the sky as an opal-coloured dawn began to spread across the city. It was easier to see, now, the spread of devastation. Even from this panoptic altitude, the screams and yells could clearly be heard. The ghost took them south again. They approached the Tower of London, set like a carved block of silver in the cement of its moat. In the main courtyard, and out into the main thoroughfare, Beefeaters were fighting with Zombies. Several were aiming rifles and blasting the creatures in the chest – with little effect. One or two were flourishing their halberds. But Scrooge could also see that several of the red-and-black jacketed soldiery had changed their notional diet from beef to brain, and in the main approach confusion was the military order of the day.

The ghost brought Scrooge straight in to the open windows of the royal apartments. They stopped upon the balcony there, and Scrooge saw Her Majesty herself, as round as a Christmas Pudding wrapped in black crêpe paper. She was sitting upon a low settee, and the Imperial Crown itself was set upon a cushion on a low table beside her.

An equerry burst through the door. 'Ma'am! Terrible news!'

'Is it time to go to the Abbey for the Christmas Morning service?' Victoria enquired, equably, of the equerry. She indicated the crown. 'The warder of the Crown Jewels has readied the necessary.'

'We are under attack.'

'Attack?'

'I fear so, Majesty.'

'Attack from whom?'

'The entire city has been taken over by some devil's monstrosity – ordinary folk turned into savages – they are devouring people's, forgive me ma'am, people's *brains*.'

The Queen's poise didn't falter. 'Dear me,' she said.

'Your subjects are being murdered and devoured all around us.'

'Most unfortunate.'

'Monsters that devour the living flesh,' gasped the royal servant. 'They are being called – Zombies. Devils possess them – *use* them for evil!'

The Queen, still sitting, stiffened her spine. '*We*,' she said firmly, 'are not Zom-used. Where is John Brown?'

'Oh, Your Majesty! Horrible news. I fear your Ghillie has been possessed by whatever devilry is causing this carnage,' the equerry gabbled. 'No longer John Brown the Ghillie – now John Brown the Ghoulie.' As if on cue, there was a roar and a crash behind the royal servant. He turned just in time to see the enormously bearded face and short, stumpy body of Brown himself coming crashing into the room. 'Br-r-r-rrrr,' he bellowed, putting all his innate, Scots 'r'-rolling ability into the word, '-rrrr-rr-r-rrrRRRR*rains*!'

'Aaargh!' cried the equerry. He did his best, in his quailing, terrified way, to block the monster's access to the royal personage with his own body. But Brown had him by the throat. The Zombie struck like a cobra, biting hard into the other man's lower lip, ripping it free in a gush of blood. Scrooge could hardly bring himself to watch. He saw the back of the equerry wriggle horribly, struggling to escape. He saw Brown gobbling hungrily, and tearing the whole of the man's jaw free, spitting it away. Then the Zombie began to eat up through the roof of the fellow's mouth. The long brown beard waggled hideously. Gore trickled down it to dribble onto plush scarlet.

Through all this, Her Majesty the Queen did not move.

Brown finished with the equerry in short order, and cast his lifeless body aside. His face, white teeth flashing in a mess of blood and gobbets of flesh, was a terrible sight. He blinked, and portions of the equerry caught on his eyelashes flicked free.

'Quee-ee-eeee-een,' he growled.

He started forward.

'Brown!' the Queen said, sharply. 'Show some *prudence*, man! Call yourself a Scot?'

At this point Scrooge could not stop himself crying out, in anguish: 'Your Majesty! Your Majesty!'

'She cannot hear you,' said the ghost, in a mournful tone.

'We *must* help her!'

'There is nothing we can do.'

'But we *must*!'

But the Spirit only shook his spectral head.

A moment before John Brown reached the settee, Queen Victoria – displaying a nimbleness and rapidity surprising in one of her girth and age – hopped to her feet. As Brown stretched his neck forward and opened his mouth to bite into her, Her Majesty caught up the Imperial Crown, raised it swiftly in both hands, and brought it hard down upon Brown's dolichocephalic head. She put such force into the motion, in fact, that the crown passed over the skull and slid, like a muzzle, or a fantastically bejewelled mask, straight over Brown's face. His roar was muffled at once, and, unable to see, he crashed into the wall. This motion drove the crown more forcefully over his head; and now it covered the entire skull tightly, like a helmet.

The Queen stepped briskly to the window. 'You disappoint

me much, Ghillie. Silly of you to act so willy-nilly,' she said, in a loud voice.

Unable to see, and unable to lever the crown from him, Zombie-Brown turned himself in the direction from which her voice was coming. Without pause, and with terrifying immediacy, he lumbered directly at her. She waited, once again, until the last minute before stepping gracefully out of the way. Brown, with a crown for a head, smashed through the glass, passed directly before Scrooge and the ghost on the short balcony, toppled over the balustrade and fell. The weight of gold and jewels brought his head straight down, and he landed – pinioned directly through the middle of his cranium – upon the upwards-spike of the railings below. And there he stayed, balanced upside-down so exactly, and counter-weighted so heavily by the crown, that his legs continued waving to and fro and his arms flopped. From inside the helmet came a moan. It was not properly audible, although the likelihood that it was a reiteration of the word *brains* is, I suppose, high.

Through the air they flew, man and Spirit, and below them, all through the long Christmas Morning, Scrooge watched the mayhem develop. The Metropolitan police, called out in force, struggled to contain increasing masses of Zombie assault. Scrooge and the ghost flew low over Holborn, where dozens of blue-uniformed men struggled with ranks of mouth-agape monsters. There is only so much a man may do against a deathless, implacable, superstrong foe when armed with but a whistle and a foot-long wand of wood. Scrooge watched in horror. Manfully the constables stood, and manfully they fell. Zombfully they got up again; or some of them at any rate. When those that still stood saw their comrades turn against them many gave up the fight as a lost cause, turned tail and sprinted off.

'The police are powerless to hold back the advance!' cried Scrooge.

'Indeed,' said the ghost. 'Though constabulary duty's to be done, to be done, the Zombies have the policemen on the run.' For some reason he repeated the last three words an octave lower. Perhaps he was mulling over the alarming implications those three words imparted.

They flew across the more salubrious districts – Islington, Highbury. Houses whose doors were adorned with Christmas wreaths – Christmas trees visible in gaudy splendour through their parlour windows. But havoc had entered in. The sound of breaking glass, carol singing interrupted with shrieks of terror and dismay, church bells ringing half a peal, the chiming breaking off and only human screams remaining.

'This house,' said the Spirit, bringing Scrooge low, 'is familiar to you, I think.'

They alit upon the roof of a spacious house – and Scrooge knew it for that of his nephew. Through an open attic window they glided down into the main room. There was a tree, dressed so as to embody the same relationship to a forest tree as a scarlet woman does to a nun. Below were presents, and in the room was gathered the whole family – Fred, his wife

Hilda, and their three delightful children. And yet, despite the mound of elaborately wrapped presents, nobody's attention was on the tree. Instead, the family clustered at the various windows. 'What is happening, Fred?' Hilda asked, nervously.

'Armageddon,' said Fred, in an I-told-you-so voice. It was a striking thing, indeed, to hear a voice in which genuine fear and self-satisfied smugness were so equally mixed. 'This is the culmination of the disaster I foresaw. People did not listen to me then, but they'll listen *now*. Some terrible madness has possessed people, that they wreak such violence on life and property. See! See! Is that not Robert Haydon, the vicar of Saint-Cuthbert-in-the-Wold, staggering down the street with his arms out? And is that not the head of Thomas Carlyle, the noted essayist and historian, dangling by its beard from his hand?'

'Horrible!' gasped Hilda, putting a dainty hand to her mouth.

'Let's see! Let's see!' cried eleven-years-old Charles. His sister, aged nine, was struggling with him for the best view, crying: 'You've had a long look. It's my turn!'

'Avert your eyes, family,' declared Fred. 'Across the street the milkman is devouring the brains of our neighbour, Mrs Baille von Edda.'

'Oh, *wow*!' cried the eldest child. 'Look at the blood!'

'I want to see too!' cried his sister. 'Dad! It's not fair! Charlie won't let me see the devouring!'

'Want see!' put in the youngest child, three-year-old Algernon.

'Dad! He's had *ages* to look! It's not fair. Mum, make him let me have a proper look!'

'You've seen,' objected Charlie.

'Not a proper look. I only saw a *bit* of blood.'

'I saw blood *and* brains,' gloated Charlie.

'Want see blood!' said little Algernon.

'Children,' said Hilda, gathering her three offspring into the embrace consisting partly of her arms and to a greater degree of her crinoline, and moving them away from the window – to their expressive vocal disappointment. 'It is not a sight for tender young eyes. Fred!'

'Yes dear?'

'Fred, I am scared.'

'My darling,' said Fred, standing tall. 'There is no need for alarm. I am here to protect you, and I shall not leave your side. These monsters may be roaming outside, but we are safe within our house – and this, our home, is as good as a castle. The doors are locked and bolted, the windows secure. Best of all, we have all the supplies and necessities to last a lengthy siege – all the food and drink for a hearty Christmas season. Though this disturbance is severe, I cannot believe it will last long. It must burn itself out within a few days, and then order will be restored. So let us enjoy Christmas as well as we can. Starting with a Christmas breakfast!' He went to the speaking-tube embedded in the wall, rang the bell to the kitchen, and put his mouth to the orifice.

'Cook? Ah, Cook. We are ready to take breakfast now, if you please. What will you be serving us?' He put his ear to the tube, and listened, the spoke into it again. 'Very good. With some fried mushrooms, perhaps. And a little egg.'

Fred turned back to face his family. 'Wife, children. The cook is frying up some brains – calf brains, I daresay – and I have asked her to do some mushrooms and eggs as well. Perhaps a little kedgeree. We shall have a splendid breakfast. And afterwards we will all open our presents.'

The children danced with joy at this prospect, linking arms and ring-a-rosing about their mother.

'You see, my dear,' said Fred, to his wife. 'There is no cause whatsoever for fear. I am here both to protect, and to provide, for you. I am your knight, your champion, your trusty sentry and your doting lord. No matter how terrible things become, I shall shield you from h—'

As he was speaking the Cook came into the parlour. She did not exactly open the door to do so, unless the phrase 'an open door' can be taken to include doors in which the panels have been smashed out, and the bulk wrenched from its

hinges. The Cook stood in the doorway, blood smeared across her three chins. She was holding the bleeding severed arm of the under-butler, still in its olive-green livery and dripping red from its ragged end.

'—Aaaaarm!' shrieked Fred. He put his head down and ran full pelt across the parlour towards the window, diving straight through an instant hailstorm of glass fragments and dowels of wood. Outside, on the lawn he somersaulted head-over-heels, but didn't lose momentum: he was back up on his feet and running fast. As Scrooge and the ghost got to the window they saw him jink left to avoid the milkman, and vault an iron railing in one bound.

'I have,' said the ghost, carrying Scrooge once more into the air, 'one more house to show you. Do you know where your clerk, Cratchit, lives?'

'The Borough, I believe,' said Scrooge.

'Have you ever been to his house?'

'Not I, ghost. I am ashamed of the fact, but I never took interest in his doings. I wish I had been less selfish.'

'We shall observe how honest Terence is celebrating,' said the ghost, 'this Christmas Morning.'

'O ghost! *Must* we see more horrors? My eyes are sore from weeping at the monstrosity I *have* seen. I have been a miser and a misanthrope – I have sealed myself away from human company. But I shall do so no longer. If I survive this awful day – if humanity itself survives – I shall dedicate myself to ...'

'Here we are,' said the ghost, brightly.

They had crossed the Thames and were descending upon the higgled-piggled rooftops of the Borough. Borough High Street ran straight as a tree-trunk towards the south. Here was the Marshalsea prison – a crowd of desperate good citizens were clamouring at the main gate to be let in, for sanctuary against the evils outside; but the turnkey, with the support of the prison population as a whole, was denying them ingress. Zombies staggered towards the mass of humanity from every side.

Down a narrow side street, and touching ground again in a dingy court, Scrooge and the ghost stood before the Cratchits' home: narrow, dark, but clean. The door was open, and Scrooge stepped tentatively inside.

There was no sign of life. 'Have they all been slain?' asked Scrooge. 'Why is the house empty?'

'It is not empty,' said the ghost.

Through the poky hall and down a step into the house's back parlour. Inside, in a low wooden chair, sat the slumped form of Tim. He was actually fairly tall – which is to say, he was *tiny*, much as Robin Hood's John was *little*. As he sat in the chair – wait, let me be clear. The reference is to Robin Hood's *companion*, the *man* called John, who was known as Little John despite being a fellow of some stature. I did not mean to make reference to any, er, *portion* of Robin Hood's body. Nor, of course, did you think I was making such a reference. Of course not. This is not the place to speculate on the proportions of any aspect of Robin Hood's anatomy. This is the place to note that 'Tiny Tim' was, actually, if anything, a little on the tall side. To be frank, and with the benefit of hindsight, I might wish I hadn't introduced the Robin Hood analogy at all. Might we concentrate, please, upon Tiny Tim?

With his skinny stature, and his face ravaged by illness – the cheekbones accentuated by his thinness, the eyes tightened and thinned by mump-like swellings – he looked simultaneously young and old. His crutches were together, leant against the wall beside the chair. He was asleep. 'Or,' asked Scrooge, peering closer, 'is he dead?'

'He has been near death for a long time,' replied the ghost. 'But he still breathes.'

Scrooge looked around the parlour. 'And the rest of the Cratchits?' he asked. 'It is true I have not paid much attention to my clerk's life – I shall undertake to be a better employer, and a better man, in future. But I believe he has four children, does he not? Where are they? Where is his goodly huswife? He himself?'

In the tiny kitchen through at the back something was clucking, like a chicken. Scrooge peered through and saw it was the lid upon a saucepan of boiling water: the noise was caused by steam forcing the metal enough to escape, and the lid slapping back down into place. The potatoes inside had turned almost to soup. Scrooge moved it from the heat.

'Scrooge,' said a voice from the parlour.

Scrooge stepped back through. It was Tim: waking from his death-like slumber, he had opened his narrow little eyes and was peering at the guest. 'You can see me, little master?' asked Scrooge, amazed.

'I can see you.'

'And do you know me too?' asked Scrooge, amazed.

'Of course I do.'

'Of course? But I have never visited this house in my life before.'

'No,' said Tim, in a distant, almost ethereal voice. 'Unlike your partner, Nathan Marley.'

Scrooge could not suppress a shudder. 'My former partner,' he muttered.

'Mr Marley was a frequent visitor, and a frequent bestower of charity,' said Tiny Tim. 'Though very ill himself – ill fit to die. Yet did he not abandon his charitable visits.'

'A good man,' said Scrooge, feeling conscience-stricken, and not liking the feeling.

'Did he,' asked Tim, in a strange, almost trilling tone, 'visit *you*?'

This drew Scrooge up short. 'What do you mean?' he demanded.

An eerie smile was flickering about Tim's mouth, and his narrow little eyes closed to two hyphens. 'He came to see you, and now you come to see me. But it is too late.'

'Too late?'

'It is Christmas Day! You should have come yesterday – or earlier.'

'I do not know what you mean,' said Scrooge. 'Although perhaps you seek to rebuke me for my lack of prior charitable activity. It is truly, though not kindly, spoken, if so: and all I can say is that, in the future I shall make up for what I failed to do in the past.'

'The future!' chuckled Tim. 'The very idea!'

'I assure you, little sir . . .'

'There is no future. Did you not hear me say you have come too late? You do not remember our conversation, in that antipodean refuge?'

'You confuse me, sirrah,' said Scrooge, uncertainly. 'But perhaps your mind is itself muddled by your illness. Where are your parents? Your siblings?'

'I sent them out,' said Tim, opening his narrow little eyes. 'I can call them back, if you desire to meet them.'

'There is great danger in the town,' said Scrooge. 'You – and they – must leave. I have money. I'm sure we can escape.'

Tim began laughing again. 'It is like talking to a backward child.'

'Hold your tongue sir!' snapped Scrooge, stung by this rudeness.

'Of course, you could not come any earlier,' said Tim.

'Because you—' and he flicked a glance at the ghost '—could not manifest on any other day.'

'No more,' said the Spirit, 'than you could bring about this destruction on any other day.'

'Wait – he can see *you too*?'

'They are coming, Spirit,' said Tim. There was an eldritch quality to the figure – something incomprehensible. If it is true, as the poet says, that the child is father to the man, then this sickly child seemed grand- or great-grandfather. 'They are coming,' he said, 'and they are hungry.'

'I don't understand,' said Scrooge.

The sound of footsteps in the hall outside. The low moaning of the familiar word: 'brains' 'brains'.

'We have to go, right now, Mr Ebeneezer,' said the Ghost of Christmas Present, in a state of considerable agitation. 'We really must.' They went towards the parlour door, but as they did so Zombie-Cratchit appeared. Behind him was Mrs Zombie-Cratchit, and three little Zombie-kiddies. 'No way out there.'

'Can somebody please explain . . .' Scrooge said.

'I'm a little busy right now,' said the ghost, scanning the parlour. Two tiny, high windows provided illumination; but there was no other exit. 'I don't see that I'll get you through those,' he said, meditatively.

'Ghost . . .'

Zombie-Cratchit and Mrs Zombie-Cratchit, in their eagerness to devour Scrooge's brains, had both attempted to come through the parlour door at the same time. It not being wide enough to permit this, they had become temporarily wedged. 'Braains!' they cried, in unison.

'We have to get out of here,' said the Spirit. 'And since I can't take you through the wall . . .'

'How is it that Tiny Tim can see you, when nobody else in London ... ?'

'Or perhaps I *can*,' said the ghost. 'Scrooge, flick open the door of the oven. In the little kitchen there.'

Scrooge, the puzzled expression never leaving his face, leant in and yanked the door. The coals inside had burned a long way down, but were still blue-white hot.

'Toss in that bottle – that one,' said the ghost, indicating a large and well-corked china bottle of medicinal spirits. 'Be sure to shut the door again.'

Scrooge did as he was bid, pushing the door closed by pressing the scalding handle with his foot.

'And *under* the table we go,' sang the ghost. 'Now!'

In a jumbled tumble Mr and Mrs Cratchit broke through the doorway and piled into the parlour. Scrooge let out a little 'eek!' and dashed under the table. There was a monstrous bang. A wave of heat and pressure washed through the room knocking Mr and Mrs Zombie-Cratchit backwards in a heap upon their Zombie-offspring.

'Come on,' cried 'the ghost'. 'I'm really extremely *keen* to get out of here – they'll eat me just as quickly as they'll eat you, you know. Quicker, actually; because they don't have to break through any armour of bone.'

Scrooge, coughing, a little stunned by the detonation, was, however, in possession of enough of his wits to a sufficient degree to follow the ghost's instruction. The crumbly bricks of the back kitchen had been caved out by the blast, and Scrooge picked over the rubble easily enough. Masonry dust had lodged up his nose – but it mattered not, because the ghost caught him by the forearm and lifted him into the air, just as Zombie-Cratchit, emerging through the ruins, lunged for his leg.

The sun was low in the sky. 'My time with you is almost over,' said the ghost, gently lowering Scrooge through the air and onto the ground in the empty expanse of Leicester Square. Blank facades of window and brick watched the scene sightlessly. Several corpses lay sprawled with that indolent horror that only corpses possess. The sounds of moaning – always the same syllable – drifted on the wind; but there were no Zombies in the immediate vicinity.

'I don't understand anything of this,' said Scrooge, bitterly.

'My brother, the Ghost of Christmas Future, will explain everything,' said the Spirit. He seemed immensely wearied. An unpleasant odour was emanating from his ectoplasm – or whatever it was that composed his body.

'Such horrors ...'

'There have been Zombies before, in human culture,' said the Spirit. 'Earlier variants of this same Zombie plague. Humanity has recorded the monsters thereby created in fact and, more distantly, fiction: Grendel, Frankenstein's creature. But never until now – not until today – has there been a variant of the plague so virulent that it spreads as rapidly as we have seen today.'

'Ghost, you said I was immune. How can that be?'

'My brother has the answers,' said the Spirit, in an exhausted voice. 'Remember that this is ground zero. This city, on this Christmas Day, in this year. The other occasional outbursts of the plague could be contained – can be contained. This is the variant that must ...' and his words faded, as his very outline softened ' ... be ...' his very form dissipating, melting into an indistinct cloud ' ... stopped ...' he said. And he lost all coherence, falling to the hard ground as a rain of urine that splashed Scrooge's shoes. 'Ugh!' said Scrooge. 'Oh, now, really that is *too much*.'

Rather than remain vulnerable in the open, Scrooge slunk into the shadows at the corner of the square. He stood shivering in the evening light, glancing anxiously about for Zombies. But when movement came it was of a different sort: the shadows about him appeared to be shifting, to be roiling and coiling, and then – three yards from him – to be coalescing into a human form. This, Scrooge thought, as the eerie sense of uncanny manifestation crept up his spine, this must be the second Spirit.

THE SECOND SPIRIT

'Oi-oi,' shouted the second Spirit. 'Re*sult*. Ow-ow-ow. *Wicked*.'

'I beg your pardon?' said Scrooge.

This Ghost of Christmas Future manifested a very different appearance to his brother. Black clad, unwigged, younger and more obese. His face was pale, and as transparent as his brother's, but his trousers and top, and the hood that flopped between his shoulder-blades, possessed a different sort of transparency: the half-glimpsed through-seeing of shadows.

'Yo!' he called. 'Scrooge. *Mister* Scrooge! *Master* Scrooge! *Yo* the man!'

'Hello,' said Scrooge.

'So my bruv took you on the full ay-ay-ay aërial open-topped-bus Maj. Myst. *Tour* of the capital, yeah? AMIRITE?'

Scrooge blinked. Then he blinked again.

'Christmas Pres? My bruv, yeah. Wiv the *wig*, an that? *Wicked*.'

'I'm sorry. I really have no idea what you are saying.'

'Don't sprang me, dude! It ain't nah-nah that youz clear-speaking yourself, blood, you get me? I coming and all the git-gonny, what wiv Corner at the sic o'clock, the left hand round the houses – dig? Ombre ombre, I ain't no hollerback, is the,' and he made a strange downward flicking gesture with his right hand, '*main*, *line*, fo-sho *mainline*, yeah? Yeah? You *got* me?'

'I,' said Scrooge, pausing for twenty seconds or so, during which time he made a concerted mental effort to apprehend what he had just heard. 'No,' he said, eventually.

'For the jam of shoreline!' the Spirit said. 'When you hang with a necker, you hang – yeah? Ain't *no* ting, cept when the gin-a-body ups the 808, you get me? But where *are* the snows of yesteryear? U, G, L, I, you ain't *got* no alibi. *Yo* the *slow*. AMIRITE?'

'If you're asking me whether I consider what you say to be ... right,' said Scrooge, with the air of a man rather too obviously clutching at straws, 'then, I ... eh.'

'Nah, nah, nah, nah. My bruv done been done gone. I can see wiv eyes, and the third, the third. There's a bacon on the bush, there's a chris that crossed, dig dag dug. Speak-n-spell. Get low in the ghetto, the lies buried in da library, ouch!-ouch! is the hierophant of an unapprehended futurity – *word*! Crow, that box is *righteous*. Man! Oo. Above all, enframing conceals that revealing which, in the sense of *poiesis*, lets what presences come forth into appearance. And *well* wicked, man, well *wicked*.'

'Man?' repeated Scrooge, uncertainly.

'Ain't no corners on a circle, du-uu-ude!' said the Spirit. Then he made a series of very high-pitched squeaks, like a mouse. Then he said: 'Chutney! Chutney!' and looked hope-fully at Scrooge.

'Well,' Scrooge replied, eventually. 'It certainly has been a colder than average winter.'

The Spirit sighed. With a brief shake of his head he fished a small book from the inside pocket of his coat. Scrooge saw upon its cover the title: PHRASE: DIG?

The ghost opened the book and looked closely at the first page. 'How,' he said, after a minute or so. 'Are. You?'

'Very well, thank you.'

The Spirit scrabbled through the leaves, ran his forefinger down a page, and seemed pleased. 'I Am,' he said, 'The Spirit Of.' He stopped, and glanced up. Scrooge looked expectantly at him. He returned the look, just as intently. Scrooge tried waggling his eyebrows a little to encourage him. The Spirit scratched his head. Then, with a little start, as if realising that he had forgotten something, he looked down again and said, 'Christmas Future.'

'Pleased to meet you.'

'In the,' said the Spirit, and he made a round, sweeping gesture with his right hand, 'Future, We Speak Different. Lee. To. You.' He didn't seem happy with his articulation, and so traced the line again with his finger. 'Lituyu,' he said. 'Diffren. Lituyu.'

'I comprehend you very well, now, sir.'

'For me,' said the Spirit. 'Your Speech. Speesh? Is Also Strange To Me. Being an. Tick waited.'

'Naturally.'

'But With the Aid of this Book,' said the Spirit, still reading from the page, 'Of Phrase. Of this Book-of-Phrase. You and I. May Com. May Com. Maycom.' He tutted himself, took a deep breath, and essayed the whole word at a rush: 'Commu-u-une. Ick! Hate!'

'Very well,' said Scrooge. Less certainly.

The Spirit looked up, looking rather pleased with himself. 'Oi-oi, yeah?' he said. 'Ya dig me? "Ick!" "Hate!" Yeah?' He didn't wait for Scrooge to reply, but put his head down and once again rifled through the pages. 'I will Show *You*,' he said, 'the Future.'

'The Future,' repeated Scrooge.

The Spirit nodded briskly, and tucked the Book-of-Phrase away inside his coat. Then he held out his hand.

Scrooge took a deep breath. Then he took the proffered hand. In a different sense of the word 'took', obviously.

Scrooge was expecting to fly up in the air, as he had previously done with the Ghost of Christmas Present. But for long seconds nothing at all happened; and then, rather than fly up into the sky, the sky descended to *them*. It was a very striking and peculiar experience; but Scrooge was certain that neither he nor the Spirit moved. Yet the street flew away, as if brushed into a void. Scrooge felt as though he and the Spirit had been thrust into the darkness between the very stars. There was nothing at all around; they were surrounded by blackness. Then, out of the perfect opacity, deep purple sparkles began to throb and burst. These strange northern-lights colours brightened and increased in intensity, and then – with such velocity and on such a scale that Scrooge flinched – a luminous green pulse flared up directly in front of them. It stretched to a line and twisted like a snake, until it made the unmistakable shape of a gigantic S. Scrooge looked at the ghost for some explanation of this bizarre phenomenon, but as he did so the S flew past them and vanished into the dark and backward abysm.

'Spirit—' Scrooge began to ask. But as he spoke a second green pulse flared, and twisted, this time forming a gigantic C. That letter also hurtled towards them, such that they passed right through its crescent. 'Spirit?' Scrooge asked. 'What is this? These . . . letters. What do they signify?'

'Ask the hand,' the Spirit replied, mysteriously. 'This ain't my regular clockin-on. Ouch! Nowsah. Got a kushti Saturday job, man, at *Game Station*. Fight tha Power! Yeah! This just me filling in for a mate who had to go to the hospital for a thing with his insides, wap-a-doodle, his duodenum as it goes, ya dig me?'

A third letter began to form – a more complex folding of luminous green light.

It was an R.

'SCRAM, I reckon,' opined the Spirit, nodding. 'It's some vermicious k-*nidd*ery.'

But in this the ghost was mistaken, for the fourth letter – as it formed – took the form of a gleaming snake that curled about to bite its own tail. As this shining O formed, and solidified and then hurtled towards them Scrooge saw that another had already shaped itself behind the first, and a third behind that one. Scrooge and Spirit passed right through the middle of each in turn. And there was a yawing sensation of motion inside Scrooge's stomach, and in the instant they were hurtling along a corridor formed by an endless succession of gleaming green and blue and purple hoops. The blood pounded in his ears: duh-duh-duh-durr, duh-duh-duh-durr, duh-duh-duh-durr. And yet, even as he rushed inside and along this weird spectral capillary, Scrooge could not be sure that *he* was the one in motion. Perhaps he was still stationary, and the structure was somehow moving *around* him.

'Wee!' cried the Spirit.

'Bah!' coughed Scrooge.

Without warning the glowing circles that constituted the tunnel dissipated, the last one breaking like luminous suds into a ζ and falling away. Scrooge, blinking, looked about himself. He was still holding the half-palpable hand of the

second Spirit; but the darkness had gone. They were surrounded by light. He gazed about him to gain his bearings
and saw that the light was the colour of pale blue silk, and
that there were white shreds above him. 'Clouds,' he said.

'Dahn, man,' said the Spirit.

Scrooge looked down – and there was London. He recognised the snake curl of the Thames, shining in the sunlight
like metal, and the spread of roofs. His point of view shifted,
although once again without any accompanying sense of iner-
tial shift in his body, such that it was not so much that he flew
over the roofs of his home town, but rather than the panorama
slid away below. The city scrolled from north to south, and
in the streets (the Spirit brought him lower, or else the whole
earth tilted up higher, so that he could see in more detail)
were nothing but Zombies.

Scrooge gasped.

In every thoroughfare, dressed in rags – or in some cases
their scrawny bodies quite naked – the Zombies walked. They
bumped into one another heedlessly, and knocked themselves
against walls and other obstacles, but nothing interrupted
their tireless perambulations. Down the line of the north road,
through Smithfield's open square, along past the dome of
Saint Paul's and over the river the perspective moved – only
Zombies. With nothing to feed upon, with nowhere to go and
no purpose to their lives, they still stumbled and wandered.
From time to time one of the creatures would open its mouth
and the familiar horrid syllable would emerge: 'Braa-aains.'

Scrooge turned his face to his conductor. 'Has everybody
become contaminated by this Devil's plague?' he asked in an
anguished voice.

'Check it,' said the Spirit, gesturing with his free hand.

They were passing over Wimbledon Common. The
Zombies were sparser here, although a few made their way

over the hillocks and tufts of grass. The Spirit directed Scrooge's glance. A bush, green as pistachio in the winter light, was shaking and jerking. The Spirit brought Scrooge lower and he could see that the plant was a piece of disguise. It lifted and moved, because it had been fixed in order to camouflage a hatchway. The open hatch revealed an excavated tunnel beneath; and for long moments there was no further motion. Then, as tentative as a meerkat, a human face poked up. Almost as soon as it had appeared it ducked down again. The sound of a scuffle proceeded from the hole. The head bobbed up, looking displeased with its altitude, and then ducked down again. Scrooge, his ears still able to detect the sound of Zombie moans on the wind, leaned closer to the hole and overheard the following exchange.

'I won't go!'

'If you don't go we will all starve!'

'Perhaps I prefer to starve!' declared the fellow. With a start, Scrooge recognised the voice – and put it together with the face he had seen moments before, although thinned and stretched into a distanciating caricature of itself. It was his nephew, Fred. Was poor Fred now reduced to lurking in a dug-out to escape the Zombie hordes?

'Perhaps,' Fred keened, 'I prefer starvation to the death I would meet with . . . up there!'

'Make that choice for yourself,' declared Fred's interlocutor. 'Do not make it for everybody else in this refuge!'

'If other people want rabbit,' said Fred, his voice audibly breaking, 'then other people can bally well go fetch rabbit!'

'The rota has come round to your name.'

'The rota be dashed! Rota? *No* sir! The rota can *swivel*!'

'When we accepted you into our sanctuary it was on the understanding that you would take your part in the rota. We cannot survive without food!'

More voices could be heard from inside the shelter: 'Go on!' 'Be a man!' A particularly deep growl: 'Gertcha!' Then Fred shot up from the hole like a cork ejected from a pop-gun. As he scrambled around on the turf, Scrooge watched the hatchway close again and the bush settle into its space. Fred twisted his head left, right, glancing about the landscape blinking in terror. Then he crawled hurriedly back to the hatch. 'Let me in! Please, I beg of you!'

From under the ground, like the ghost of Hamlet's father, a muffled voice replied: 'Fetch food, and you can come back in.'

'I,' gabbled Fred, 'I *have* got food. I popped round and collected it. I've got *loads* of food. Armfuls of it – open up.'

'You must think,' replied the ground, 'that I was born yesterday. You haven't had time to check any of the snares, or anything! If you're going to try and bluff your way back in, at least leave it a few minutes before you hammer on the hatch.'

'Gnah!' ejaculated Fred, in frustration. The situation evidently could not be helped. He got onto his feet, in a crouched-down posture, and scurried away from the mound.

Scrooge, and the Ghost of Christmas Future, followed.

Fred really did look in a poor way. His once expensive clothes were in tatters and rags. Which is to say, they were rags. They were, as it happens, both in rags and rags. Fred's twitchy manner and cowering, cringing manner was as ragged – in terms of the dignity of human behaviour – as his clothing. He ran alongside a hedgerow, and crawled on all fours to a set of rabbit snares. There were three rabbits in the nooses of wire, dead, and Fred – evidently eager to collect food and return to the subterranean safety of the hide, leapt forward with a barely suppressed mutter of joy. But as he approached, all three rose and hissed, lurching towards him with their little bunny teeth snarling. Only the tether of the snares held them back, and with a squeal Fred skidded and backed off.

He dived behind a bush and hid there sobbing for long minutes. But soon enough a larger fear of remaining out in the open overcame his timidity and he set off again, looking for other snares. And – audibly thanking his lucky stars – he did so, after only a minute or so: one dead rabbit, its neck bent in the noose. Fred found a stick, and spent some seconds poking the beast – but this one had died before catching the plague. Fred unfastened it and tucked it into the crook of his elbow. 'I'm a hero,' he muttered. 'I alone braved the Zombies – the greatest and bravest man left in this miserable land!'

It was time to return to the lair. He got to his feet, turned in the direction of home, and let out a shriek that sounded rather like a piglet with its tail caught in a mangle.

Before him stood a Zombie's swaying figure. 'Braains!' cried the monster.

Fred turned about again, and stretched his long legs to run as fast as he possibly could in the other direction. But his first step landed in the noose he had just emptied, and, although his second step worked well enough, his third brought him up close with a wire tight around his ankle. He sprawled forward, the dead rabbit hurtling from his hands, and his front teeth bit into the turf. 'No!' he shrieked, wriggling around and trying, with shuddering fingers, to loosen the snare. The Zombie advanced upon him.

Then, glancing up, Fred's eyes were caught by something. 'Hilda?'

The Zombie, looking down, halted. It swayed, uncertainly.

'Why does it stop?' Scrooge, asked of the ghost.

'Like,' returned the Spirit, 'shingle in the start-up, yeah?

So-so slow-mo, and calling dawg to the *re*call, yowser, let-me-hear-you-say *AY*-oh, *AY*-oh. You dig me?'

'Never mind,' said Scrooge.

'Hilda?' Fred was saying, from his supine position, shading his eyes with his right hand to get a better view. 'Is that . . . is that *you* my darling?'

'Braains,' returned the standing figure, although in a smaller voice.

'It is I, my love! Your husband! However horribly this Zombie plague has attacked your soul, my darling, you surely cannot have forgotten your husband?'

'Hus . . .' said the Zombie, uncertainly.

'That's right, my sweet! Just so my love! Do you remember the day we married? That wonderful day in Saint Cedric in the Cellar's? Your dress was as white as your porcelain skin, Hilda, how beautiful you looked! And do you remember how nervous I was? It was the greatest day of my life; I wanted so badly not to get anything wrong. So nervous! You remember how, as he fumbled for the ring, my best man accidentally trod upon my foot, and how I, reflexly, punched him on the nose? He hit his head on the font going down, you recall? How you tittered, as he bled out upon the aisle!' Fred slipped a wheedling tone into his voice, getting to his knees, and looking up at her with imploring eyes. 'You would not devour *me*, Hilda my love? You would not devour your *husband*?'

'Hus . . . ?'

For a moment the Zombie that had once been Hilda swayed a little, her lips working soundlessly. She gazed down upon the figure before her. Then her mouth opened. 'Hus . . .' she groaned. '*Brains!*'

'No!' squealed Fred, falling back.

'Husbrains! Husbrains!'

She was on him like a ferret on a snake, and Fred's screams, though intense, were shortlived.

'Dawg!' said the Spirit. 'We'd better split to the max, you *get* me?'

⁕

They rose into the air, and continued their passage above a desolate landscape. They swept over southern London. The Marshalsea, once a prison, had become a refuge of life – although its beleaguered inhabitants – Scrooge saw as they passed, in the yard and leaning from upper windows – were close to the final starvation. Scrooge and the Spirit glided over Croydon, that palatial and luxurious suburb, richer than Babylon and more beautiful – but now reduced to a parade of shambling monsters.

Over Kent they flew, leaving London behind.

'Where do you take me, Spirit?' said Scrooge.

'You need to *upgrade*, my made-man. Word. Speech ain't-should be out of reach, yeah? Rah, rah, like Square be*ware*, you dig? To the maxx. We going global, master-blaster. Globe. Al. Ch'*mawn*!'

'That the garden of England,' said Scrooge, sorrowfully, 'should become the graveyard of England.' On the positive side, at least the fresh air seemed to be having a good effect upon his cough.

They passed over the noble edifice in the heart of Canterbury, the medieval-built Cathedral that had stood proud over the east-Kentish marl for many centuries. Now its main tower was blackened and hollow. Thousands had flocked here, hoping to find a divinely protected sanctuary from the oncoming Zombie advance. But the ancient stones had proved but poor defence, and in the final bloodbath candles had been kicked over, tapestries had flared, and the whole had erupted in fire. Now, through the narrow lanes of the ancient Cathedral city, Zombies moved.

They flew on, over fields run to weed and tumbledown villages, until – in the distance – Scrooge saw the glint and greyness of the English Channel. They flew above the bone-white cliffs of the southern coast and circled in upon Dover Castle. The walls of this fortress were guarded with soldiery, and the streets surrounding it thronging with Zombies, pressing in a great flood upon the walls. From time to time the soldiers fired down into the mass, but it seemed as pointless as firing arrows at the ocean.

'Oi oi,' said the Spirit, pointing. They were sharing the sky with a large zeppelin-balloon, still distant over the Channel, but moving through the aerial medium by means of two large propellers, and coming closer.

'A flying machine,' said Scrooge.

'Future, innit.'

The Spirit brought Scrooge down upon one of the castle's upper balconies, and the two slipped in through an open window. Inside sat Her Majesty, surrounded by a dozen ferociously armed bodyguards. The months had slimmed her frame down considerably, and as a result she looked more drawn and tired than the last time Scrooge had seen her. More strikingly she was wearing not the black dress of fond memory, but an all-leather ensemble. Scrooge thought of asking the Spirit the meaning of this strange garb – but thought better of the impulse, and instead attempted to puzzle it out for himself. 'Presumably,' he thought to himself, 'it is the better to protect her against the chance of Zombie bite.'

A courtier – dressed not in the usual finery, but likewise in a jacket and trousers of leather – hurried into the room. 'Your

Majesty, the zeppelin-airship of the French Third Republic has been spotted approaching. It will be here in a quarter of an hour.'

This seemed to create a great buzz in the room – grins breaking out on hard-worn faces; hand shaking hand and shoulders being slapped. 'Good news, Your Majesty,' said a white-bearded fellow in a general's jacket. 'After a year, your escape is secure.'

'I take no pleasure from the thought that I am abandoning my kingdom,' said Victoria, in a slow, dignified voice. 'Nor that I must perforce leave so many of you behind me.'

A murmur rolled about the room: 'no, no, Your Majesty, never think of it.'

'Worse, my dear subjects, my dear friends! I grieve that my escape will constitute merely a temporary reprieve. For though the Continent be presently Zombie-free, yet can it remain so?'

'Your Majesty!' cried a voice. The crowd parted, and a handsome, frock-coated man stepped forward. 'Your Majesty I have news – hopeful news, on that score.'

'Yes, Faraday?'

'Ma'am, I know that some in this room,' and Faraday looked about him, 'consider my year-long experiments to have been nothing more than wasted time. And I am the first to concede that most of what my team has attempted has proved fruitless. But yesterday a man was brought to us – brought through the Zombies by the closed carriage . . .'

'With loss of life amongst my men,' growled the white-bearded general.

'A most rare and unusual individual, Your Majesty. He is the first we have discovered to possess an immunity to the Zombie plague. He has spent a fearful year, lurking in shadows, eating scraps, avoiding the violence of the monsters.

But although he has been repeatedly exposed to the plague itself, he has not become sick! If we can isolate the antidote to the sickness from this man's blood . . .'

There was a murmur.

'Another false dawn, Professor?' said the general. He was mopping his brow with a white handkerchief. Exhausted, half-starved and worn out with a year's unstopping assault, he was clearly at the end of his tether.

'Not this time, ma'am. I am certain. Would you permit me to present the gentleman to you, before you leave upon the airship? It might give your heart hope to consider that you leave behind, not despair, but a fighting chance!'

'Present him by all means,' said the Queen. 'But the French airship is only ten minutes away, and the pilot will not, I'll wager, be persuaded to linger. I must depart as soon as it is here.'

The scientist made a gesture, and one of his assistants ducked out of the room. In a twinkling he returned, bringing with him – Scrooge himself.

'Me!' said Scrooge. 'Ghost, how can it be?'

'You got me, brother, you got me. The low-down's no show-down.'

'Don't you *know*?'

'Know's a no-no, Mr Seldom Sam-I-Am-Urai. This *ain't* my timeline, dig? You think I could even *exist* in this waste-land? How could I have got the wisdom? Ain't no Wandsworth Further Education College of Art, Music and Design in *this* versy-vice-a version of events. What-what?'

Scrooge looked in wild surmise from his doppelganger to the spirit. The other-Scrooge was thin and bald, dressed in workman's clothes; but there was a vigour in his old limbs and an unmistakable glint of steel in his eye. He carried a rifle over his shoulder but surrendered this, as necessity demanded, to one of the bodyguards. Standing before the throne he bowed, stiffly.

'Long live Your Majesty,' he said.

'Thank you, Mr . . . ?'

'Scrooge, ma'am.'

'Scrooge. Are you related to the celebrated eighteenth-century Pirate, Scally McScrooge the Rouge?'

'My maternal great-uncle, ma'am.'

'Some of his courage has been passed down to you, I see.'

'It has not been an easy year, ma'am. For myself – or for any of us who survive. But I have learned much about the monsters. I have learned how to avoid them. And I have learned how to slay them, although that is still dreadful hard to achieve.'

'Professor Faraday thinks a cure might lurk in your blood.'

'I only pray he is correct, ma'am.'

'Your Majesty,' cried a leather-clad courtier. 'The airship has landed! The French ambassador craves an audience.'

Momentarily the Queen's brows contracted. 'Show him in.'

'The French ambassador?' growled the general. He mopped some more at the sweat on his brow. 'He, here? What is *he* doing upon the transport? And why does he wish an audience?'

'You look unwell, General,' noted Victoria. 'Pray, sit down.'

The general was lead to a chair by the wall. 'If he offers to insult you, ma'am.' He muttered. 'I'll . . . I'll . . .'

'His Excellency Le Comte de Frou-Frou, Ambassador to the Republic of France,' cried a crier. A tall, well-dressed man entered the room. As the crowd of people parted around him, he strode purposefully towards the Queen, bowing with an elaborate flourish. 'Your Mazhesty,' he said. 'I regret to inform you that zhe French President as been compelled to postpone is offer of sanctuary.'

As one, the whole room gasped.

'Postpone?' repeated Victoria, drily.

'Wis the greatest regret. As you know, it as only been wis the greatest of efforts dat zhe Continent of Europe has been kept Zombie-free. The coastal defenses are on i-alert around zhe clawk — for boats continually wash oop, and corpses floating in zhe wash are rare-uh-ly as dead as zay seem.'

'Yes?'

'It as been decided that zhe risk of permitting any immigration — even of a personage as exalted as yourself, Your Ighness — is too great. Zhe Republic of France regrets ziz painful necessitay, and begs you accept zhe cargo carried ere by this airship as a gift: food, wine and ammunition. It is being unloaded as I spik—'

'You swine, sir!' came a voice from the crowd. An angry buzz passed through the room; but the Queen held up her hand.

'Whilst regrettable,' she said, in a calm voice, 'we of course understand France's decision. Convey our thanks to your masters for the gifts you have brought us, and our regrets that we cannot thank him in person.'

The ambassador bowed again, as the angry murmur spread once more about the room.

'Gentlemen!' he cried, as he straightened himself. 'Believe me truly sorry at the news I must convey! But you yourselves must accept, all of you who guard your Queen with such steadfast valour, you must accept that in all likelihood the Zombie plague has already breached these walls! We *Cannot* risk carrying it to the Continent!' He turned to face the Queen once again. 'My sympathies are heartfelt, Your Highness.

How does the English phrase go? My heart goes out to you – ueh – urgh!'

This last syllable, which was neither French nor English, was uttered as the Comte's facial expression twisted in pain, and his chest bulged forward. There was a wrenching, sucking sound, accompanied by the snapping of bones. With a popping sound his chest literally broke open – blood sprayed, pieces of bone burst and flew, and a red glistening, sopping mess emerged, poking itself towards the royal throne.

Held in a superhuman grip, the ambassador's still beating heart was forced out of his body, towards the Queen.

Behind him stood the general, his face now a mask. His white beard waggled and a word emerged: 'Braaains!' He released the heart, so that it tumbled into the carpet before the royal chair, and bit hard into the back of the ambassador's neck.

The entire room was shocked into silence for a frozen moment: but then the crowd roared into life. Three guards interposed themselves between the Queen at the point of danger, caught her up and hurried her through a side exit. Others unholstered firearms with celerity and directed a fusillade of shots into the head of the new Zombie. Its body twitched and jerked under the impacts, but it was not distracted in its fell purpose.

Confusion reigned: men yelling. Gunsmoke billowing, the noise of weapons discharging was deafening.

The Ghost of Christmas Future tapped Scrooge on the shoulder. 'Time to climb,' he said, looking up at the sky through the open window. 'You dig me?'

'But . . .' said Scrooge. 'Her Majesty . . .'

'Viczombia,' confirmed the ghost, offhandedly.

They flew up until little peaks and dents of the wave-vexed waters became smoothed to grey, and the channel became a broad textured plain separating England and the distantly visible margin of France. The sun's reflection lay upon the surface, a felled column of brightness. On the roof of Dover Castle, where the zeppelin-balloon lay, tied by its tether, like a giant pale slug, men struggled with Zombies. 'Like ants on the deck,' was the opinion of the ghost. 'Like *ants* on the *deck*. Sweet.'

'Is the Queen lost, Spirit? Has she survived a whole year only to fall, moments away from rescue? Is there any hope for Albion?'

'You asking, fool? I sing no *choir* to your enquiry, you get me?'

'Does that mean you don't know?'

The Spirit pulled a series of elaborate facial stretches and contortions, so pronounced that Scrooge momentarily wondered if he were having some sort of fit. But his face settled again, and he only said: 'Yeah.'

They flew higher. The last Scrooge saw, the Zombies had reached the zeppelin.

'And what happens to me, in that castle?' he asked.

The Spirit, though, was fiddling with a strange hand-sized pellet of metal, upon which a series of tiny illuminated squares were visible, each containing a different sigil or rune. Scrooge peered at the single word written along the top: iTARDS. 'We need to blast a *master* fast-forward, innit – spin me *right* round,' he said.

'Ghost, tell me this,' Scrooge asked. 'Earlier you said that, although you are showing me the future, it is not a future that you yourself call home.'

The ghost looked at him, nodded rapidly, smiled, and

said: 'Nah idea, man. Nah idea what you're on about. Speak English, oi?'

'This future,' said Scrooge, slowly and loudly, 'is not *your* future?'

Understanding bloomed in the ghost's eyes. 'Like, wiv the time-line, and the *spine* line and the which-is-yours-an-*mine* line, yeah? I gets you, Old Geezer. It's a puzzle-o-monkeys, that's for sure.'

'I had not thought of it before,' said Scrooge: 'for why should it trouble my thoughts? But now that I am caught up in these strange adventures, it occurs to me that, if time is like a path, along which a traveler may hurry forward or turn back, to travel into future or past, well then, may not time as a landscape not be a whole *network* of paths, each mapping out a slightly different cause-and-effect? Why atoms themselves,' Scrooge continued, warming to this theme, 'might be made to roll down one or other path, as light itself pours from the sun. And maybe the great rainbow curve of gravity itself is actually the trajectory of all these individual atomic split-paths along the multiple pathways of time. Am I anywhere near the truth?'

The ghost looked impressed. 'Well, even though you were born, fo-sure, couple-centuries too early, still, man, I gots to say,' he said, warmly, 'you know your Hawking.'

'Am I?' said Scrooge. 'I rather thought my cough had started to get better, actually.'

'Scope the spoke,' said the ghost, pointing. The zeppelin had lifted into the air from the roof of Dover Castle, although it was listing noticeably to the left and was trailing mooring ropes and cables. Zombies were clinging fast to the webbing about the main balloon.

'We got to gets,' said the ghost, pushing a sequence of keys on his little device.

At once the strange hoops began to form in the air before them, and soon enough they were rushing through this spectral tunnel – or, as before, they were motionless, and the tunnel was moving *around* them. 'Where to now, Spirit?' Scrooge called.

'Through the Channel Time Tunnel, Bo! Bo!' returned the Spirit.

O followed O, but this journey seemed briefer; and the last O broke up into a LA and a smaller LA, as Scrooge and the Spirit emerged over the French coast.

'Gracious!' gasped Scrooge.

'Monster, innit?' said the Spirit.

The entire coastline – it seemed – had been turned into a vast fortification: beaches walled and fenced with shard-wire; clifftops bristled with cannons, and crenulations. Huge castles nestled in bays. As the ghost took Scrooge east along the coastline of the Pas de Calais they passed over coastal villages converted into military bases – harbours in which enormous dreadnoughts were docked – it was a Hadrian's Wall for the late nineteenth century, a vast network of bulwarks and defensive positions to keep the Zombie threat at bay. To keep, Scrooge could believe, the British Isles penned in. Had his homeland been totally overwhelmed? What happened to Her Imperial Majesty?

'Ghost,' he asked. 'Can it be true that we are now further in the future?'

'Narst. Ee,' returned the Spirit, apparently in confirmation.

'The machines of future war-making,' said Scrooge, 'are astonishing. Flying zeppelins is one thing. But that dreadnought there,' he pointed to a huge barrel-shaped craft, 'is literally a giant floating cannon! It must be a thousand yards long! How mighty the shell that such a device could propel.

And that! What hideously beweaponed piece of ordnance is *that?*'

The Spirit made great play of consulting his phrase book, nodding, and then putting it away again. Shortly he said: 'That's the latrines. For the barracks, you get me?'

'But where are the *soldiers* to operate these mighty machines? Where the sailors to crew these dreadnoughts?'

'Reckoo-oon, blood. Reckoo-oon.'

They swept lower, over a complex of grey stone walls and redoubts: stone-clad bunkers through which poked cannon-barrels like broom handles. There was no sign of life. They flew on, towards the harbour: the ironclad battleships rocked slowly from side to side at anchor; as if shaking their mighty metal heads in answer to Scrooge's question.

'There!' cried Scrooge. He pointed: on the lengthy stone groyne, which is absolutely the correct technical term for a stone pier that stretches out to sea at a harbour such as this, a man was walking. But as the ghost drew Scrooge through the air towards this figure it was soon apparent that this was no living man.

'*Cervelles!*' the creature was moaning, his arms before him. '*Ce-e-ervelles!*' He was dressed in the dark blue of what had once been a military uniform – but now was ripped and besmirched. 'But what does *cervelles* mean?' asked Scrooge; and then, instantly answering his own question, in a sheepish voice. 'Although actually I think I can deduce the answer from the context.'

'I'm going with *servile*,' said the ghost, flipping buttons on his iTARDS. His spectral face took on a disappointed expression. 'Wrong? *Toss*clumps, man.'

'*Cervelles!*' gasped the Zombie.

He staggered on. He was, it seemed, in pursuit not of a person but rather a seagull. The ungainly bird, gawky and scrawny, was leaping a few yards ahead of the beast's approach, repeating the gesture as needful. From time to time it gave voice to its fingernails-upon-the-blackboard cry. 'But if this Zombie is reduced to chasing after seagull-brains ...' Scrooge speculated, aloud. 'And considering how little seagulls are renowned as deep thinkers ...'

'Don' look good,' agreed the Ghost of Christmas Future.

The Zombie was approaching the end of the groyne, a word which, let me remind you, is indeed and genuinely a harbour-related piece of vocabulary. The seagull leapt-hopped a yard along the pier; the Zombie staggered on. The seagull hop-leapt, and the Zombie staggered on. The seagull hop-stepped, and the Zombie stepped into the vacancy after the pier's end. For a moment, whilst its back foot was still on solid ground, it teetered. Then, as it started to tip forward, and with no hope of stopping itself, it wailed one word – '*brine!*' – and splashed into the sea. With a gloop, it disappeared from view.

The seagull unfolded its wings, shook them a few times in a desultory fashion, and soared away.

The ghost and Scrooge were left to the desolate and empty harbour, with its idle military hardware, and the tireless heave and push of the sea.

'So this is the Christmas of the future, is it?' Scrooge asked, looking about at the desolate scene.

'Dawg,' confirmed the Spirit.

They left the coast and flew over the French countryside: derelict villages and untilled fields. Zombies were rare in the open fields, but their staggering, shuddering forms were easy to spot walking about the streets of the cities. Scrooge was prepared to believe that the entire world had been devoured by the plague – but then they passed over the broad, shining boulevard of the Rhine river, bright white in the winter sunlight. On the far bank the signs and symptoms of civilisation began to emerge. Smoke threaded into the air from chimney pots. People could be seen in the fields and roads.

'The Rhine has evidently become the new battlefront between humanity and this terrible plague,' noted Scrooge.

'You what, blood?' asked the ghost.

'Never mind.'

They swept down, low over a bustling military camp. Troops, each man swaddled improbably in massy padding, bolsters and leather, and sporting enormous helmets wholly encompassing their heads, were drilling; others in the same over-engineered protective garb were attempting training exercises – climbing walls, struggling under barbed wire. The sheer bulk of their outfits slowed them down, although presumably experience had taught them that speed could profitably be sacrificed for protection.

They swept over a lengthy brick-built barracks, and beyond it they came to a series of bungalows – officers quarters. On the verandas some men stood reflectively smoking, and others stood looking westward, towards the Rhine and the wasteland beyond it. As they passed, Scrooge could see the careworn faces, the burden of command intensified by the knowledge that the very literal survival of humanity depending upon holding this line.

Finally, they touched down outside a bungalow at the far end of the encampment. The Ghost of Christmas Future stepped through the open door, and Scrooge followed. He was almost beyond surprise, after the extraordinary and terrible things he had seen, to see – himself, sitting in a chair, polishing a rifle barrel. Sitting opposite, fitting together the components of a pistol of unfamiliar model, sat another man in his middle years. This man's countenance seemed oddly familiar to Scrooge, although he couldn't quite place it: a high brow, large round eyes propped on two sets of pouchy bags, a long, thin, well-formed nose and a square-trimmed goatee beard affixed to his chin like a hairy epaulette. 'So, Scrooge,' this man said. 'Though we've shared this bungalow now for more than a week, I feel we haven't properly got to know one another.'

'There's been so much to do,' agreed alter-Scrooge. 'Maintaining a constant state of military readiness is an exacting business.'

'The defence of humanity itself against the Zombie horde,' said the other. 'You never told me how you came to escape from jolly-old England?'

'I came over in a small boat,' said Scrooge. 'I didn't expect to find the coastal defences in such a state of disrepair. I suppose I planned to try and talk my way through. In the event that proved unnecessary.'

'But how did you cross France, and evade the Zombie population?'

'A trick, Dickens, that I picked up in Blighty. First catch an as yet uninfected small animal, one capable of some glimmer of thought. I was lucky to find a little dog in the fields outside Calais: a bright little thing. I put him in a cage, and put the cage on the end of a pole. Then – and this was the tricky part – I found a Zombie horse. Since I don't advise you try and saddle such a beast, I'd recommend finding one already in harness. There were plenty of old army beasts staggering about northern France. Then it's a simple matter of hopping on the thing's back, poking the poke forward like a knight's lance such that the cage and its occupant dangles before the horse. It's better than a carrot to a donkey. Better not least because Zombie horses do not tire, or become distracted. The beast galloped without pause straight to the German border.'

'Extraordinary! You might think the horse would prefer *you* to some dog in a cage?'

'You might, I suppose. But then again you might assume the donkey would prefer the sack of carrots across its back to the one dangling in front of its nose. And yet . . .'

'True. And the dog?'

'It's about here somewhere. They call it Scroogie *Doux*, I understand. On account of its sweet nature.'

'Remarkable.'

'And you, Dickens?' asked Scrooge, sighting along the barrel. 'How did you escape?'

'Oh I came over to the Continent long *before* that dreadful Christmas Day when the plague broke out,' replied Dickens, examining the fat-barrelled pistol he held in his lap. 'I was over here with an, eh, female friend. My wife and I being separated, you understand. When the full state of the emergency became apparent . . . and especially after that blasted airship brought its cargo of Zombies upon an unsuspecting coastline, I volunteered. The United Continental Army was keen to take me – even though I'd no prior experience of the military life.'

'What did you used to be, before this catastrophe?'

'I was a writer – a teller of tall tales. Perhaps you have heard of me?'

'I was never a reader of popular fiction,' said Scrooge. 'I regret to say.'

'No matter. If I ever survive these events I'll have the material for a novel like no other, and no mistake. And you? What did you do before these events overtook us?'

'I worked in the City of London,' said the alter-Scrooge.

'Trading bonds, lending money. I call it work; in fact it was a disgraceful form of sanctioned miserliness.'

Scrooge, standing in the corner of the room beside the Ghost of Christmas Future, barked out: 'Hey! Bah!'

'Terrible though it has been, but this Zombie Catastrophe has been the making of me, as a man. I live for others now, instead of myself; and although it has been hard – and sometimes hair-raising – I have known a fulfilment and inner peace that money never brought me. You might say,' he went on, 'that this has been a form of Zombie Salvation. Scrooge the miser redeemed by the intervention of unearthly and supernatural manifestation.'

'Is it true what they say of you?' asked Dickens, looking straight at his companion with bright, unwavering eyes.

'What *do* they say of me, Dickens?'

'That you are immune to the plague.'

'That's the truth. I know it for a fact because a Zombie – an old partner of mine called Nathan Marley – bit me. On the posterior, no less. But I have suffered no Zombification from this assault.'

Dickens had a little notebook down and was scribbling. 'You don't mind?' he asked. 'Always good to keep notes of intriguing stories. M-A-R, Ellie-why, and what was it? Jay, ay, see, oh, bee. Dead, yes. Did he attack you in the street?'

'He came into my apartment, actually. With his jaw hanging open!'

'And how is it that you are immune?'

'I cannot say. Our best scientists have examined me, and taken phials of my blood – but to no effect. I fear our science is not yet advanced enough to make use of the protection Providence has, somehow, placed upon me. As to its purpose, or my eventual fate, I am in the dark. All I know is that, since that bite, I have known a vigour and energy previously alien to me.'

'A lucky circumstance,' agreed Dickens. 'Is your name spelt with a J, or a G?'

'The latter.'

Dickens made a few more notes, and put his notebook away. 'I must say,' he sighed, 'I will be surprised if I ever have the leisure to write another tale.'

'You are pessimistic, then, about humanity's prospects?'

Dickens got up from his chair and stood by a window, holding the fat gun in his right hand and looking out upon the world. 'When the Zombies were contained in the British Isles, and given their aversion to swimming, we stood a chance. But if the plague could breach so wide a defensive ditch, can we truly believe that the Rhine will hold it back?'

'As you say,' said Scrooge. 'The creatures mislike the water. We must thank the almost wholly mindless nature of fishes, I suppose.'

'But one may stumble upon a floating raft, a tree, an abandoned boat, and float over by chance.'

'True. But *we* yet live,' said Scrooge, also getting to his feet. 'And with life, hope. I am, for instance, pleased to have had the chance to get to know you, Dickens. We have had *fun*, have we not, in this bungalow together?'

'All manner of fun,' agreed Dickens, smiling.

There was a loud thump from behind one of the bungalow's doors. Both men spun to face it: somebody, or something, was in the building's back room. 'Who's that?' called Scrooge. 'Who's there?'

Silence. Then another thump. And then the unmistakable groan – 'braains!' – and an almighty splintering crash, and the door fell apart.

'Dickens! Zom– *In* the bungalow!' yelled Scrooge.

As the shambling figure lurched through, the Ghost of Christmas Future took hold of the arm of Scrooge (*our* Scrooge) and pulled him back through the door. 'Inda bungalow,' he was muttering. 'That's too much, man. Split is *it*, ya get me?'

On the veranda of the low-slung house, Scrooge glanced back through the main door just in time to see Dickens levelling his fat-barrelled pistol, and firing directly into the face of the approaching Zombie. Its skull dissolved into a red and brown mist, blown backwards to layer the wall behind with the force of the explosion. Dickens himself was knocked backwards and almost fell.

Outside, there was immense commotion: officers and men running in every direction, and a great deal of shouting in all the languages of Europe – French, German, Italian, Polish, Russian and Greek. An adjutant came running full pelt up to the doorway of the bungalow, hooting: 'Captain Scrooge! Captain Scrooge!'

'What is it?' returned the alter-Scrooge, emerging from the house. He was spattered with a mess of red – a fact that made the adjutant step back in shock. 'Captain Scrooge! The Zoms have breached the river, sir!'

'*How*, in the name of all that's holy, have they done that?'

'They walked over it! I know it's hard to believe, sir, but – they simply *walked*. And sir . . . some of them are armed.'

Dickens had emerged also, and the two men stood side by side, looking grimly at this news.

'Armed?' snapped Scrooge. 'What do you mean? Talk sense, man!'

'Some of them have picked up incendiaries – infernal devices. They have not made these, of course; but they seem to have some distant inkling of what they can do. From time to time a Zom explodes a bomb as he is carrying it . . .

advertently, or inadvertently, who knows? But he spatters, eh,' the adjutant went on, looking nervously at the mess of Zombie blood upon Scrooge's clothing, 'spatters his infectious material over a wide area. The worst thing of all is that they have never displayed this sort of behaviour before . . . .'

'Indeed,' agreed Dickens. 'It is a malign development that they seem to be acquiring the use of tools. Perhaps they are . . . Oh, what's that newfangled term?'

'Evolving?' suggested Scrooge.

But at this Dickens looked puzzled. '*Evolve?* What's that?'

'It's the,' said Scrooge. Then he said. 'Do you know, I'm not entirely sure. Something to do with baboons, I think. What word did *you* mean, then?'

'I was thinking of *machinists*.'

'You think they have developed this capacity off their own bat?' Scrooge asked.

'What do you mean?'

'Perhaps they do not act entirely alone. I sometimes feel – I know not why, exactly – that some mastermind, some evil genius, directs their actions.'

'At any rate, they must be stopped,' said Dickens. 'We will need to muster the men. *Behind you!*'

'Behind *me*?' replied the adjutant, at whom Dickens was now pointing. 'I'm not sure it's a good idea to have *me* lead the men into battle sir. Wouldn't it be better for *you* to . . .' But in the very middle of this sentence, and as realisation dawned, the adjutant's voice dropped to a low and rather mournful tone '. . . oh you mean *behind me* in the sense of . . .'

He tried to spin about, and to draw his holstered weapon at the same time; but the Zombie was right at his back – a snarl, a flurry of yellowing teeth, and the man went down in a spurt of his own blood. He did not, to his credit, yell out. Dickens steadied his pistol, and Scrooge his rifle, and together the two men fired at the floored and struggling twosome.

'This place get toasty,' said the Ghost of Christmas Future, looking about nervously. 'Did my bruv ex*plain*, in the *main*, how Zombies got a special yen love ghost food? Pure mentition; it's sugar-sugar to their unkind *kind*. Yeah?'

'He did,' said Scrooge.

'Up, blood.'

As the two of them rose into the air, leaving the camp a confusion of struggling men and monsters, Scrooge said: 'Do you know what, ghost? I believe I am starting to comprehend your futuristic lingo.'

'Gib to the er,' the Spirit replied. 'An the er to the *ish*.'

It was only as the ghost led Scrooge through the sky in a wide arc that he understood what the ill-fated adjutant had meant about the Zombies *walking* across the river. In the depth of a central European midwinter, Christmas ice had formed upon the wide and fast-flowing river. Given that the creatures had not managed a crossing previously, Scrooge assumed that no such freezing had occurred in the five years leading up to this moment. But it was an unusually cold Christmas Day. The margins of the river were frozen solid; and the central channel of dark flowing water had been slowly shrinking upon a plate-ice mantle. It had not yet wholly sealed, but there were enough free platforms of ice, bumping from jag to jag, to serve as crossing points.

The Zombies were coming.

Some of them were simply advancing as of old, with their arms out and their mouths chewing their one relentless, remorseless word. But others had indeed picked up weapons — grenades and bombs.

The United Continental Army hurried to ready itself on the far bank, the front-line soldiers impeded by their bulky protective gear waddled like toddlers. Guns were mounted, and aim taken. One officer, mounted upon a froth-mouthed charger, rode desperately up and down the lines, his sabre raised high in his right arm. 'They are coming, men!' he yelled, into the clear winter air. 'They are coming! But we are ready for them! We are ready to repel them – with our guns – and our bombs – and ... and ... our *bombs* – and our *guns*. Zo-ombie! Zo-ombie!'

And the men took up the war-cry together. '*Zom*bie! *Zom*bie!'

From the advancing mass of their enemy, only a dolorous uprearing din: *bra-a-ains* from some; *cerve-e-elles* from others.

To the rear of the position a mighty cannon discharged its shell with a roar and a cloud of gunsmoke. The shell, spinning upon its horizontal access faster than a teetotum, clove the air directly between Scrooge and the Ghost of Christmas Future, and set up such *tourbillons* of wind that the two creatures whirled and span through the air like an autumn leaf.

'Time to make ourself scarce, like,' opined the ghost.

Scrooge looked down and saw the shell explode upon the white of the frozen river: a mighty blast of white turned ice to steam, and great chunks of ice flew through the air. Some Zombies flew also, and others tumbled into the black waters.

The ghost pulled Scrooge up and away from the trajectories of the shells.

Below, the first wave of Zombies was approaching the defensive positions. Rifle fire crackled and spat; mortars gobbed their incendiary parcels, and spikes of flame forty feet long spewed from nozzles. At first this fusillade had an impressive effect: rank upon rank of walking dead tumbled in a tangle of fire, or were disassembled into a rain of still twitching and groping body parts. From time to time fire or cordite engulfed one of the Zombies carrying bombs, and they flew into the air in all directions in a dazzling firework blast.

But the Zombies had numbers on their side, and nothing daunted them. The big cannons did their best to break up the ice, the gun positions drizzled bullets down upon the advancing mass in a steady flow. But the Zombies continued to advance.

Soon enough the assault built up and began to penetrate the front line. From his elevated, godlike perspective Scrooge was happy he could not hear the screams of the dying. 'They cannot hold the line,' he said, 'against so unrelenting and populous an assault!'

'Word,' said the ghost.

'Is humanity then doomed? Must the entire globe be covered in this tide of death and horror?'

'Let's check it, yeah? You get me?' The ghost was jabbing his forefinger at his little machine, and once again the great Os began to form in the sky. This time, however, they signified only a mighty wail of lament for the great army being crushed and devoured on European fields below them.

They hurtled along the tunnel with an even-greater seeming velocity. The flicker of passing brightnesses dazzled Scrooge's eye. 'Long way south-east,' the ghost yelled, 'and a longer way to the future – dig?'

'I see,' bellowed Scrooge in return.

'May take – a–shabba! Shabba! – a little longer than usual.'

On they zoomed.

Scrooge tried to picture a map of the world. If neither a mighty river like the Rhine, nor even the English Channel, could halt the advance of these hellish monsters, then what could? Europe lay open to them – and over the steppes into Russia, and the whole of Asia. There had been plans under discussion to excavate a canal separating Asia Minor and Africa – widely discussed in the papers – but Scrooge assumed such ambitious engineering works had been shelved in the face of the catastrophe. Accordingly, the Zombies could walk easily across the deserts into Egypt and so spread through the whole of that vast continent. And once they had threaded their tireless, restless, onward-marching way through the forests of Siberia, only the icebound straits of Baring stood between them and the Americas. Could the brave American soldiers defend against the onslaught, in harsh winter conditions, on the open ice?

'I doubt it,' Scrooge said to himself.

They were emerging from the last of the hoops now, and floating down through a milder air. 'It is warmer here,' Scrooge noted. 'Spirit, is this a future Christmas Day, as the others were? Or have you brought me into a summer world for once?'

'Nah, it's Christmas Day, boom-boom-shay-shake-daroom. AMIRITE?'

'Has the world's climate altered in some radical way, that the sun's heat scorches the middle of December?' Scrooge looked down upon a desert land, waste and empty. 'Where is this place?'

The ghost looked vague. 'Dundee? Glasgow? Edinburgh? One o dem.'

'Scotland?' gasped Scrooge, in horror.

'Perth,' said the ghost. 'That's it. Perth.'

'Has *Scotland* been so disfigured? Has that beautiful land of mists and dark heather been transformed into this neo-Arabian wilderness?'

The ghost looked at him as if he were an idiot. 'Nah,' he said. 'Nah-nah. Don't shake *that* milk. Australia, innit.'

'Australia?' gasped Scrooge.

'Ya.'

'Australia! Imagine that! And what is the year?'

The ghost checked his strange little tablet. 'Today we're going to Perth – see – like, it's eighteen ninety-nine.'

'Eighteen ninety-nine,' mused Scrooge. 'It has such a futuristic sound! And am *I* still alive in this distant future?'

'Scroogie,' said the ghost, affectionately. 'Scrooge, E. Scrooge, E. Scrooge, E.'

They came to land in the broad main street of the Australian town of Perth. It was late in the afternoon, and very hot. A few people – real, human people – were out and about, but most, evidently, were keeping themselves indoors until evening's cool. At the far end of the street were two large sentry boxes, bewreathed with fat barbed wire like metallic holly; and between them stood a jagged tapering device – a rocket of some kind – pointing at the sky, and ready to be launched at the earliest news of a Zombie attack. Two soldiers stood guard, armoured like futuristic centurians – no longer weighed down with the bulky swaddling Scrooge had seen on the banks of the Rhine; now their armour was sleek, close-fitting and black, topped off with a helmet pronged with two stubby Viking horns and a black cape.

'Of course!' said Scrooge. 'Though the rest of the world fall to the Zombie plague, yet Fort Australia may survive, surrounded by water on all sides, and spacious enough to accommodate the whole as-yet uninfected population of the world!' He gave vent to a musing humour. 'And what wars have been fought in the Malaysian peninsula? What bravery and sacrifice is holding back the hordes? I can only wonder!'

'You coming, dawg,' asked the Spirit, 'or what?'

He was standing before the door to a large, rather imposing house.

'And we are going inside?' asked Scrooge.

'Is the Pope a Zombie? Of *course* we're going inside. Come on.'

Through the front door they stepped into a cool, marble-floored hallway. Across the chessboard pattern, past a sonorously ticking grandfather clock. There was a smell that Scrooge took, at first, to be incense; but which – as the two of them ascended the main staircase – he realised was more specifically chemical: the smell of a laboratory.

'What house is this, ghost?'

At the top of the stairs the Spirit of Christmas Future turned to face Scrooge – and the latter noted a change in the spectral countenance. He looked tired; old. 'The long day wanes, innit,' he said. 'End of a century, end of an era, end-y dependy comes out the play.'

'It is as it was with your brother,' said Scrooge, sorrowfully. 'Your have nearly exhausted your time.'

'Main line, fo-sho, you got me,' agreed the Spirit, wearily.

'Ah! We are finally communicating. So, with your last energy, you have brought me here? Yes? To some important purpose?'

'Bang the broccoli, gate-up da water. Ru-u-ude.'

'Right,' said Scrooge, slowly. 'See, just when I thought I was starting to understand your argot I am brought down to earth.'

'Chutney!' agreed the Spirit.

Across the upper hallway was a door, ajar, and through this the chemical smells of the scientific laboratory wafted. Scrooge stepped to the threshold and overheard a conversation between two men. He recognised one of the voices – with a sense of the world turning strangely upon a pivot he realised that he recognised it because it was his own.

'Now that the entire world has been overrun ...' he was saying.

'You are too pessimistic, Scrooge,' replied his interlocutor. 'And unscientific. The most we can say is: to the best of our knowledge, the rest of the world has been overrun. But we cannot be certain. Absence of evidence is not evidence of absence.'

'The silence of the telephone lines, and the radio waves?' said Scrooge. 'The complete lack of refugees, coming to these shores? The impossibility of survival in a Zombie-dominated landscape?'

'You survived.'

'I am a special case, Wells, as you know very well indeed.'

'I agree it is *likely* that Australia is the last refuge of humanity,' said Wells. 'I only insist that a scientist does not extrapolate wildly where evidence does not exist. We don't know what pockets of human survival there may be.'

'After so many decades?'

'Who knows? More to the point, we are here, still alive, still human . . . and we have had enough of a respite to develop the necessary scientific breakthroughs!'

Scrooge (*our* Scrooge, I mean . . . let us call him: Scrooge the Original) put his head round the door. Inside was a single, lengthy high-ceilinged room absolutely packed with scientific equipment and paraphernalia. There were flasks and casques, frames and flames, batteries, capacitories and various this-and-thatteries. Van Der Graaf Generators like metal mushrooms littered the bench; test tubes bubbled; and – imposingly – a huge device was set in the middle of the floor. This machine (for so it will be convenient to refer to it) was a red-leather upholstered chair, with a vast vertical parasol at its back, and a variety of ornate brass- and steel- piping and other fittings feeding into some sort of engine at its front.

There were, Scrooge the Original saw, three – not two – individuals in this laboratory space. One was, of course, himself, but much older – his head bald and freckled with liver spots, his face as lined and wrinkled as a crumbled ball of paper. He was thin, his hands trembled somewhat – yet was he still hale, and still the light of purpose shone from his old eyes.

The other man was younger, smaller and tubby. He was also bald, but with the shiny pate of a youthfully receding hairline, not the desert-scalp of a man in his dotage. He wore a pair of round glasses; the lenses shone like sixpences in the light of the laboratory.

The third figure was slight, and younger still. It was hard to see what he looked like, for he was busy with some technical assemblage, and bent over a bench at the back of the room.

'It is remarkable to me,' the elderly Scrooge was saying. 'I seem to find myself, time after time, billeted with writers.'

'When has it happened before?' asked Wells.

'Decades ago – back when the Zombies first broached the Rhine, in old Europe. I served, then, in the United Continental Army, and was in digs with a writer called Dickens.'

'I know him!' said Wells. 'At least, I know *of* him. Didn't he write *The Pickwick Papers*? Boz, they used to call him.'

'Lost to us now, alas. Infected by the plague.'

'Boz a Zom? What a loss!'

'And now,' elderly Scrooge said, 'you, my dear Wells.'

'Oh I wouldn't call myself a writer now,' said Wells. 'I've given up all that cloudy brainwork. It won't help humanity now. Much better to apply myself *practically* – what good would it have done to have written a story about a time machine? Better actually to create such a device!' He gestured at the chair-and-vertical-parasol creation in the centre of the laboratory.

'You could not have done *that* without the expert assistance of Mr Timh, I'll wager,' said the old Scrooge.

At the bench, the third figure grunted. 'And we still haven't got the propulsion quite figured out.'

Wells ignored this. 'Then I shall give you two nay-sayers another example. What good would it have done to have written a story about an inoculation against the Zombie plague? Better actually to create such a medicine. And with your blood, and the immunity it providentially bestows upon you, we have been able to do just that!' He held up a phial.

'It's no cure,' said the third figure, at the bench.

'What's that, Ni?'

Ni – by appearance a westernised Chinese or Malay man in his early youth – looked up from the bench at which he was working. 'It inoculates,' he said. 'It does not *cure*.'

'Very true,' said Scrooge. 'But inoculation is better than nothing.'

'We have preserved the whole population of Perth from Zombie plague.'

'But not from Zombie teeth,' Ni pointed out, going back to his work. 'Or Zombie claws. The fact that the plague will spread no further does not help us against the inevitability of their assault.'

'It is true,' said Wells, thoughtfully. 'And the Zombies make baffling advances against us.'

Elderly Scrooge scratched his chin. 'It is more than baffling, it is inexplicable. Think only of the numerous stretches of water separating the Asian mainland from the island of Australia, how far they have come. That they have quite overrun Vietnam and Cambodia was to be expected. And your own native Thailand, Mr Timh. But to have somehow crossed to Sumatra – to the whole Malaysian peninsula, Timor, Tonga, the many South Seas Islands.

'The Zombies *have* shown evidence of cognitive development – of a rudimentary nature, perhaps, but undeniably present. In Europe they learned to explode themselves with grenades and so spread the plague. And in the battles with the Cossacks they learned to set attack-animals upon their foe. Do you remember the dog that savaged the Czar? And the feral Zombie cat who attacked the Russian Queen?'

'*There*,' agreed Wells, 'was a cat that really was gone.'

'All that you say is true, Ni,' said elderly Scrooge. 'But

such Zombie cognitive developments have been very low-key – very *limited*. It does not explain how they are crossing these channels of water ... We must consider not only the Zombie aversion to water but also the massive military defences manned day and night? How are they doing it? Every week brings stories of another channel crossed.'

'It is almost,' Wells agreed, with a sigh, 'as if they are receiving help from amongst the human community. But who would do so appalling a thing? To doom mankind, themselves included, to ultimate death?'

The Thai scientist, Ni Timh, seemed to be taken with a small coughing fit at this point.

Scrooge the Original peered more closely at this latter figure. It was tricky to make out, in amongst the shadows, but there was something oddly familiar about the fellow. Where had he seen him before? It was a question, partly, of familiarity; but it was also a quality the young and diminutive scientist possessed – some dark charisma. What was it?

To get a better look, Scrooge slipped through the doorway and padded across the middle of the laboratory. He got halfway before he stopped. Something was not right. What was not right, he realised, upon reflection, was that everybody in the room was looking at him.

'Er,' he said, looking from face to face. 'Hello.'

'You!' cried the elderly Scrooge. 'I mean – me!'

'You can see me, then?' said Scrooge the Original. 'I only ask because I've been travelling around the world for a while now – and through time as well – without at any point being visible to its inhabitants.'

'By George!' cried Wells.

'By *Herbert* George!' said Scrooge. 'Time travel! Can it be true?'

'I eavesdropped on an earlier version of you, sir,' Scrooge

the Original said to the elderly Scrooge. 'By which I mean, an earlier version of me. In Europe, by the frozen water of the Rhine. And my point would be – I was as invisible to you, then, as I was to your companion, Darla Chickens. I mean, Charles Dickens.'

'Extraordinary!'

'What's extraordinary is that you can see me now.'

'The chronotons,' said Timh. 'The reaction of chronotonic cascade-synthesis does mean that time-particles are spilling across the room. Perhaps that interferes with the loose spectrum-refraction effect of a time-loosened body, such as this gentleman, sufficiently to render it visible.'

'Can you see my companion, too?' Scrooge the Original asked. 'He's a ghost.'

'I can only see you, sir,' said Wells. 'And I am struck by your resemblance to my friend Scrooge, here. You could be his son!'

'The Ghost of Christmas Future, he's called,' Scrooge the Original said. 'He was here a minute ago.'

It turned out that the ghost was lying on the landing, directly outside the door. He seemed to have acquired a degree of solidity, and palpability. Elderly Scrooge and Scrooge the Original picked him up between them, and brought him into the laboratory, where they laid him upon a *chaise longue*. 'He looks rather too *material – weighty*, indeed – to be a Spirit,' was Wells's opinion.

'Another effect of chronotope flow interference, I'd wager,' said Timh.

The Spirit stirred in his fever-sleep. 'Big Poppa,' he muttered, incoherently. 'Custard kipper! Hundred and thousands! Weston-super-Mare!'

'His grip upon consciousness is slim.'

'He shepherded me through time,' explained Scrooge the

Original. 'And he brought me here. I have seen the whole disaster of the Zombie plague unfold, and devastate the earth. He did it all.'

'But how?'

'A device, I believe.' Scrooge the Original slipped a hand into the ghost's pocket and pulled out the iTARDS.

All four men crowded round the little device. 'I've never seen anything like it,' said Wells.

'Perhaps it is from the future – when technology has advanced.'

'But if it is from the future,' said Wells, 'then that proves that humanity survives the Zombie catastrophe! We *must* survive, or we wouldn't be able to send a fellow like this back in time!'

'Not necessarily,' put in Timh. 'Time is not so linear. In all likelihood this individual is from a completely different time-line to the one we presently inhabit.'

'Golly,' said the elder Scrooge. 'Can we use this device to move through time ourselves?'

'I believe it is keyed to the owner,' said Timh, prodding the face of the machine with a spiderlike finger. 'It will move him, and anybody in direct physical contact with him. I'd wager we could not use it ourselves.'

'By *George*, by *Jingo*, by *John*, by *Paul*!' exclaimed Wells, suddenly, in a funk of high excitement. 'Don't you *see*? Ni, this is what we've been waiting for! You, Scrooge – and you, Scrooge – don't you see? It's a golden opportunity. You, Scrooge the second, you and your friend here, leap into the future, using your little machine. I'll rig the temporal car-burettor to the Time Machine, such that as *you* go into the future, your elder self is propelled into the past!'

'You don't mean—?' said Timh.

'I do, my dear and valued assistant! I do!'

'You misunderstand me,' said Timh. 'Do not forget that English is my second language. What I intended to communicate was that *what you said lacks meaning*.'

'Oh.'

'In order for your slingshot device to work,' Timh went on, 'the individual traveling back in time – and this weighty machine, too – would need to be counterweighted by an equivalent mass travelling into the future. The calculations would be very difficult.'

'But that need not matter. All that is needful is that we move Scrooge back beyond that fateful Christmas Day when the plague broke upon the world. It matters not precisely when, so long as it *is* before. Then with this phial of antidote,' and Wells flourished a pencil-sized glass container, 'we can inoculate the population against the plague!'

'I hate to be a wet blanket,' put in the elderly version of Scrooge. 'But that quantity of antidote would barely inoculate one person.'

'We cannot carry back imperial tons of antidote,' agreed Timh.

'That,' said Wells, 'is why *you* must go, Scroogie!'

Scrooge stiffened. '*Please*,' he said, evidently not for the first time, 'don't call me "Scroogie".'

'Listen. Before the catastrophe, isn't it true that you were a wealthy man?'

'Very wealthy.'

'And miserly?'

'Prodigiously.'

'I daresay no do-gooder, or earnest fellow looking for investment, could have persuaded you to part from your money.'

'Not I!'

'Nobody – except you yourself! Do you see? If *you yourself* came to you and explained the situation, then how could you resist the supplication?'

'But,' said both Scrooges together. They stopped. 'After you, sir,' said Scrooge the Original.

'I was only going to ask,' said the elder Scrooge. 'Supplication to what end?'

'Oh that wasn't what I was going to ask,' said the younger iteration of Scrooge.

Wells ignored this. 'You must go back, carrying the antidote with you, and persuade your younger self to release all his funds – to spend every last brass farthing he possesses – developing the science and technologies necessary to mass-produce it! The future of humanity is at stake!'

The older Scrooge sighed. 'I have my reservations, sir. How are we to persuade the general population to take this *pharmakon*?'

'Tell them it is an inoculation against cowpox! Tell them it will protect them from measles and mumps and rubella all in one go! Good Heavens man, even tell them the truth if you choose. The important thing is to place this cure in the hands of people *before it is too late*!'

'Gentlemen,' said Scrooge the Original. 'If I might ...'

'No time to lose!' said Wells. 'Come, Scroogious my old pip – into the machine.'

'Please,' said the elder Scrooge, querulously, as he was shuffled towards the chair of the Time Machine, 'don't call me that!'

'Look,' said Scrooge the Original.

'We must rouse the Future man,' said Wells. 'Timh! Fetch some *sal volatile*, if you please.'

'Be careful with him,' said Scrooge the Original, starting to feel flustered by the flurry of activity around him. 'I think he's at the end of his time – as the sun sets on this Christmas Day, so his vital power departs.'

'All the more reason to be quick. Sir! Sir!' Wells was lightly slapping the Ghost of Christmas Future about the chops. Timh brought the smelling salts over, and wafted them under his nose. As he did so, Scrooge was struck once again by the thought that he somehow recognised this Thai scientist. But there was no time to chase down the memory right now. Wells was shaking the Ghost of Christmas Future gently, crying, 'Wake up, sir! Wake.'

The ghost was murmuring something, a little indistinctly: ' . . . get up get-get-get down, nine-one-one's a prime number in *yo* town . . .'

Wells began lightly slapping face again. 'Sir! Awake! This is a matter of urgency.'

The Ghost of Christmas Future's right hand flew up, as if reaching for something on the ceiling, and his fist connected sharply with Wells's chin. The scientist straightened up very quickly, and continued the motion through such that he fell hard onto his back, like a tree being felled. Timh hurried over to him. 'He's out cold,' he reported.

'Why was that dude *hitting* me?' demanded the Ghost of Christmas Future, sitting up on the *chaise longue*. 'What's the *frequency*, Kenneth?'

'Spirit,' said Scrooge. 'Are you all right?'

'Spirograph,' replied the ghost. 'King prawn, queen prawn and the prawn princess. Locking the changes. April is the cruellest month, and February frankly has a whole S&M thing going on. Morny Stannit! Morny Stannit!'

'He's fading fast,' Scrooge said. 'His time is almost at an end.'

'Then,' said the elder Scrooge, still seated upon the chair of the Time Machine, 'we must hurry. And Wells is out for the count. Ni, can *you* operate the machinery?'

'Wells has already locked the temporal percolator to the chronoton generator,' said Timh.

At the sound of this voice the Ghost of Christmas Future opened his eyes very wide. 'It can't be,' he gasped.

'Hello, Spirit,' said Ni Timh, with a queer inflection. It almost sounded like a gloat.

'Scrooge,' said the ghost, urgently. 'Take hold of my coat. We're getting out of here, triple-quick urgent, like.'

'Wait!' wailed the older Scrooge from his seat. 'We haven't calibrated anything! I don't have the protective helmet! Don't . . .'

But the Ghost of Christmas Future wasn't about to *don't* for anyone. His fingers jabbed at the buttons on his iTARDS, and the last thing Scrooge saw was the face of Ni Timh simpering at him, as the rings formed inside the rooms and everything except those glowing circles faded to black.

In the middle of this latest journey through time Scrooge turned to look at the face of the ghost, and was alarmed to see it visibly sag and age, intermittently lit by the unearthly gleam of the passing hoops. 'Spirit!' he cried. 'Spirit! You are ill!'

Gritting his teeth, the ghost jabbed his device and the two of them re-emerged from the time tunnel. Instantly, he fell, panting, to the floor.

'You are unwell, my friend?' said Scrooge, horribly concerned, and bending down to cradle the entity in his arms. 'Why did you leave that place so precipitously?'

'Nah nah nah,' said the ghost, in a distant, feeble voice.

'It was Timh – you saw Timh, and knew him. *Who* is *he?*'

'Doobie-doobie-do,' murmured the ghost.

Scrooge glanced around: they were still in the laboratory. The windows were dark, but a weird form of gas lamp lit the whole space. The Time Machine was gone, and there was no sign of Wells – indeed, the space appeared deserted – but new machinery had been constructed. 'I assume,' said Scrooge, 'that we have travelled in time but not in space. Is that so?'

'Go go go with the chronoton flow. Nogbad the Bad. Main, line, fo-sho *mainline*. As the goatherd said when first introduced to the concept of monetary exchange: *I can't believe it's not barter*,' said the ghost.

'You're even less coherent than usual,' said Scrooge. 'Tell me: from where did you recognise Timh? Who is he?'

The ghost shuddered; he struggled, visibly, to pull himself together. He raised himself, and got, shakily, to his feet. 'Scrooge?' he said.

'Yes, my friend! I'm here!'

'That Ni – you saw him, right? He's bad news, blood. He's—' and the ghost stood upright, very straight and tall, and let out a long hissing breath between his teeth.

'He's standing right behind you!' yelped Scrooge.

'With a knife,' confirmed the ghost, in a strangulated voice. He fell forward and piled onto the floor in a heap, and lay there motionless. Behind him was Ni Timh, holding in his right hand a red-wet and dripping blade.

'Hello again,' said the diminutive scientist.

Scrooge yelped a second time, and ran to the window. 'Help!' he wailed. 'Help!'

'You'll find that things in Australia have changed since you were last here, Ebeneezer,' said Ni Timh. 'The Zombies have reclaimed it.'

In the darkened street, lit only by the moon, Scrooge saw the familiar shuffling shapes, uttering their familiar cry.

Scrooge span about. 'You!' he cried. 'You did this! You

brought these devil-creatures to this place! Why?'

Timh laughed. 'Now that's a big question,' he said. 'I'm sorry to say that I don't have time to answer it.' He bent over the ghost's supine form, and when he stood up again he was holding the iTARDS. 'I'm afraid I must be going. I'll leave you to the tender mercies of your Zombie kin. You have the satisfaction of knowing that you are the last un-Zombied human left living. As you can see, Wells's plan to manufacture a world-wide supply of the inoculation failed!'

'I knew it would fail,' said Scrooge, sorrowfully. 'For I *remember* what happened. Indeed, now that I know all this I can piece together an incident which has, hitherto, only alarmed and baffled me. I was a young lad, blithe and happy – and one evening a strange scarecrow of a man, his face disfigured and scarred, came upon me in the graveyard as I was making my way back from school.' As he spoke these words, the memory flooded in upon Scrooge so vividly that tear pricked in his eyes. 'How terrified I was! I took him to be an escaped convict, or perhaps worse – a bogeyman. He grabbed me and gabbled a deal of nonsense in my ear, about gold, gold and more gold – about how he was the only one who could persuade me to spend my gold. I, who was nine years of age! I screamed and struggled, and though he held me tight, and roared, the churchwarden heard me and came to my assistance. He in turn called on help from others, passers-by, and finally a policeman. They wrestled the old man from me – but at the last minute he lurched forward and stabbed me! I fell in a dead faint at this, but when I was awoken I found that the blade had only scratched my skin – and, indeed, barely that. I know, now, what it was with which I was stabbed.'

'Indeed,' said Ni, knowingly. He was absorbed in studying the face of the iTARDS.

'The assailant was taken away and ended his days, I believe, in an insane asylum, babbling about the end of the world and the devouring of brains. As for me, the shock of the assault was so grave that I fell into a brain-fever, and lay sickening upon my bed for a month. When I recovered I was a changed boy: no longer open-hearted and trusting, I walked through the world full of suspicion and caution. In time this calcified into a hardened cynicism about the world. I assumed it was out to get me, and so resolved to serve it in the same manner, and to do so first. I became the miser and misanthrope the world knows well.'

'All right, all right,' said Ni, looking up. 'I didn't ask for your life story.'

'I'm only surprised,' Scrooge finished, 'that my elder incarnation didn't also remember this circumstance. He would surely know that coming upon me in that graveyard would not prove a successful strategy.'

'You assume that other Scrooge was from the same time-line as you,' said Ni. 'But if he *had* been, then you and he could not have stood in the same room at the same time.'

'All these different time-lines,' wailed Scrooge. 'How it puzzles my mind!'

'Well,' said Ni, stepping over to a silver-hued machine in the corner of the lab. This had something of the look of a bicycle, although set in a steadying frame. Its wheels were solid and wires and pipes sprouted from the back of the saddle. 'I shall leave you with all the time in the world to get to the bottom of things. I have been waiting for your reappearance – with the technology available to me here there's only so much I can do. But with this!' He held the iTARDS before him. 'I have the whole of time to explore! Farewell, Scrooge.'

The body of the Ghost of Christmas Future, lying face-down upon the carpet of the laboratory, moaned. 'Ghost!' cried Scrooge, rushing over to him. 'Are you alive?'

'Barely,' hissed the ghost.

Scrooge crouched. 'Can I help you?'

'Scrooge ducky,' said the Spirit, indistinctly, into the fibres of the carpet.

'What's that?'

'Scrooge booby.'

'What?'

'Booby! Boo-oo-ooby!'

'But what do you mean?'

'Boobs!' the ghost insisted. 'Boobs!'

'He's babbling,' said Ni. He had settled himself on the saddle of his strange Time Bicycle, and was fiddling with the iTARDS. On the floor, the Ghost of Christmas Future took a deep, shuddery breath, and whispered hoarsely: 'Scrooge – duck – it's booby—' and with his last gasp he added, 'trapped.'

Scrooge had just enough wit, even after all he had been through, to flatten himself against the carpet and cover his head with his hands. As he did so the whole room was filled with a flash of eldritch light, somewhere between violet and green, and a crumbling crumpling noise. The sense of compression, or decompression, washed over him in waves, and bright blue-white flames flickered briefly. Then everything was quiet.

Scrooge looked up, and the Time Bicycle had vanished, leaving behind a patch of scorched cloth, and a rim of broken glass and cracked machinery. 'He's gone, ghost,' Scrooge said. But when he looked more closely it was apparent that his companion was dead. Not nearly dead, but actually, truly, really dead.

For a long time Scrooge sat upon the *chaise longue*, listening to the ghastly, distant howls of the Zombies in the street outside. The light burnt with an uncanny, unwavering brightness. It hung by a narrow thread, and Scrooge could not for the life of him see how enough gas was being piped through such an aperture to maintain its flame. Not that it mattered. 'The last human being alive,' he said to himself. 'I am Scrooge, none other. For there is no other kindred spirit anywhere upon the face of the whole rainy, stony earth.' Feeling a great sorrow in his heart, and experiencing that grief as weariness, Scrooge fell asleep.

THE THIRD SPIRIT

He was woken by an intermittency in the light. The flickering acted upon his exhausted, terrified half-sleep so as to make him leap, startled, from his couch. But it was only the ceiling-fitted lamp; its illumination fading as its gas – or whatever it was that supplied its power – died away. Eventually the room went dark, and Scrooge's eyes adjusted to the fainter, silver light of the moon through the window. The distant sound of Zombie moans, drifting through the night-time town, chilled him. With a belated sense of his foolishness in permitting himself to sleep, Scrooge did his best to barricade himself in: creeping downstairs to lock the front door, and then piling what he could against it. The downstairs rooms all had shutters attached to their windows, and Scrooge closed all of these, as he did with the servant's entrance. Finally he returned to the laboratory and sat upon the *chaise longue*. 'Of course it is only a matter of time before the Zombies come for me,' he said. 'What shall I do? Where shall I go? To sea, perhaps – away from the plague. Take a boat, and live on the waves. Fish for food and drink rainwater.' He laughed. 'Scrooge a sailor! The very idea.'

The laughter quickly mutated into sobs. Scrooge sat in the darkened, moonlit room, literally and perfectly alone in the world, and tears ran down his face.

✳

Eventually he slept again. He woke when dawn lit the window rose and yellow.

Tirelessly, relentlessly, the Zombies moved through the streets of Perth. 'I'd wager the best thing would be – lie low,' Scrooge told himself. 'For the moment at any rate.' He broke his fast on a tin of fruit from the house's – well-stocked – larder and diverted himself examining all the equipment in the laboratory. Whatever source of power had supplied these machines and devices had evaporated. It was presumably the same reservoir of motive force that had fed into the light that dangled from the ceiling, which (Scrooge pulled up a chair and peered at the glass bulb) whatever it was, was not a gas light. Some boiler, or generator, was no longer operational. Scrooge did not search for it. He had not the slightest idea about how to fix such a device.

Instead he lurked in the house. From time to time a Zombie banged against the door, or bumped against a shutter; but there was no concerted attempt to break in. They did not know that he was inside. If they were to find out ('and,' Scrooge said to himself, 'eventually they will find out') then doors and shutters would not hold them. He thought back to Marley, crashing through the door of his apartment back in London. A world away.

The day passed into night, and Scrooge slept. Another day, and another night.

The time sagged. The weather was warm – rather too hot, indeed, in the middle of the day, since Scrooge dare not open the shutters and let in fresh air. There were books in the library, but almost all were of a scientific and technical nature. There were weapons in the cellar, of a design and nature that were unfamiliar to him.

He tried sleeping in one of the house's bedrooms, but could not settle – the posters and drapes about the bed stifled his mind – and so he returned to the open couch in the laboratory. It was as if he was waiting for something – for some Argonaut of the time-streams to pop into the room, perhaps. For the return of Timh, maybe. Or for some newcomer. But nobody came. The longer he waited, the more his absolute solitariness impressed itself upon him.

'The last human alive,' he mused. 'Surrounded by Zombies like a pigeon surrounded by chickenhawks.' He found himself dwelling on this last image. 'So this is what humanity has become! A solitary man in an antipodean house, standing upright to say to the cosmos, I Am Pigeon. Humanity might hope for more.'

A week passed. The longest week of Scrooge's life.

The food supply would not last for ever. Scrooge began, in a dilatory and circular manner, to think of his future. He revisited his idea of fleeing onto the ocean. It did not appeal, but there seemed to be no alternative – save only loitering in this house until he starved. Or taking his own life. And Scrooge, even in his darkest moment, revolted against the thought of that.

Towards the end of the third week Scrooge came to the conclusion that it was fruitless remaining in that house. He spent long hours in the library poring over an Atlas, plotted possible trajectories across the Indian Ocean, or around the coastline of Australia. Could he single-handedly endure at sea? He who had never so much as stepped aboard a Thames pleasureboat? The first storm would sink him. But that, he thought, was preferable to the alternative.

That night he slept once again in the laboratory – for the last time, he told himself. On the morrow he would arm himself, carrying what he could in a backpack, and he would finally step out of the house, and face the perils of a Zombie-infested world.

As you might expect, he slept fitfully.

The moon was a crescent; its light turned the room's furniture into a weird collection of silver planes and blocks bordered and three-quarter swallowed in shadows black as squid-ink. Scrooge's eyes were half closed, which is the same as saying that they were half open, and his mind revolved fruitlessly on half-thought thoughts, and unthunk things. Something moved in the room.

'Zombie,' he mumbled – or tried to. But although he was awake to perceive the emotion, he was too deeply in sleep to be able to move any of his muscles. The sense of immobility, combined with the fact that there was evidently an intruder in his room, distilled a profound terror in Scrooge's heart. He struggled with his stasis, sweat starting upon his brow, and with a sense of inner release as profound as a bone breaking he leapt from the *chaise longue* and hurled himself across the room, a warrior's panic shout in his throat, his voice increasing in volume as he went: 'Raa-aa-AA-AA!'

He barked his shin painfully upon some item of scientific experiment or technological possibility, sitting inert upon the carpet. His cry changed from defiance to one of pained surprise, 'EE-EE-EE!', switching upwards in pitch by three full tones, as he hopped desperately forward through the darkness, his body inclined at an angle of forty-five degrees, on the very edge of falling onto his face. He just had time to hoot '*Damn!*' before he slapped hard against the wall, bounced backwards, and went onto his back amongst the din and clatter of a dozen pieces of smaller equipment.

A voice – thin and eerie – spoke: 'Edam?'

Scrooge leapt to his feet, irregardless of various points and places of pain about his person. 'Who's that? Who's there? Who says that name?'

'*You* spake the name, sir,' returned the voice.

'Who,' Scrooge demanded, 'who-*who*? Who?'

There was something there, something as glinting and elusive as a being coalesced from the moonlight. Its pate was bald – if 'pate' means scalp, as I believe it does, although

I wouldn't wager actual folding money upon it – its face was round as a silver penny. Little eyes like black seeds were fixed either side of a slender nose. Most remarkably of all the Spirit appeared to gleam, slightly – as if his skin were silver, and the dim light reflected from it in moony scintillations.

'A Spirit!' cried Scrooge, his terror evaporating. Or subliming, if terror be taken to be a solid rather than a liquid quantity. But going away, at any rate. 'You *are* a Spirit?'

'I am.'

'The third Spirit!'

'You were promiséd three Spirits, I believe?' asked the ghost. His voice was wayward as a night-marsh will-o-the-wisp, as warbling and piping as birdsong, as hard to catch as a greased cricket ball fired from a cannon. No, that last one doesn't work in this context, really now, does it. As, let's say, oh I don't know, as a moth flitting through the dusk. Yes, that's better.

'Do you know what?' said Scrooge; 'I *was* promised three Spirits. Right at the beginning. I'd forgotten. Or if not forgotten, then – well I rather got the impression that the third Spirit was, dead. You are the third?'

The Spirit nodded.

'You're not dead?'

The Spirit shook his head.

'Even though you are the Ghost of Christmas Past.'

'I *am* the Ghost of Christmas Past, forsooth anon.'

'Right, good. Well delighted to meet you, and, actually, now-that-I-come-to-think-of-it *where*,' Scrooge demanded, pent up fear and rage releasing in one long blast of petulance, 'have you blinking, bally, goshing well *been*? Could you not have come visit me a little sooner? Three weeks I have sat here eating bally tinned fruit and – and – living in terror every moment that Zombies would come smashing through the front door!'

There was a thud at the front door.

'Aaah!' cried Scrooge. 'No! I have alerted them to my presence with all the, you know, yelling, and lumbering about.'

The Spirit seemed to be pondering what Scrooge had said. Eventually he spoke, in his ethereal little voice. 'I could not come, forsooth, i'faith, until *this* day.'

'Could not? *Why* not?'

'Because *before*,' the Spirit said, 'twas not yet Christmas Day.'

Scrooge was disentangling himself from the various items in which he had become caught up during his desperate hopping and ungainly passage across the room. 'Christmas Day? You can't appear except upon Christmas Day?'

'Indeed, forsooth. It's true, I say. Yea, yea.'

'Is today . . . Christmas Day?'

'The moon burns blue, dead-midnight passed behind,' said the Spirit. 'The day begins anew, and Christmas 'tis.'

Scrooge looked about the moonlit room, and then he laughed, briefly and without warmth. 'What meaning can Christmas have in a world from which humanity has been purged?' he asked. 'I have been waiting, alone and in danger for chuffing *weeks*. Could you truly not have come before?'

'Only upon this day may I appear, non-nonny.'

'And why may you only . . . wait. I *beg* your pardon?'

'What?'

'What was that last bit?'

'I am not sure, forsooth, of what you ask.'

'Non-nonny? You said *non-nonny*.'

A faintly embarrassed expression passed across the Spirit's face. 'I prithee, gentle Scrooge, mock not the words/That doleful providence requires of me/Oft-time, for bulking out the lines I speak/To you, forsooth and prithee. Uh,' he waved a hand vaguely. 'Forsooth. No I said that already. Non-non.'

Scrooge rubbed his eyes. 'You *are* a Spirit, or I am dreaming. Either way – I am glad to discover that this is Christmas Day, for I had quite lost track of the calendar. The Ghost of Christmas Future – your brother – perhaps he hoped to project me forward exactly a year, but there was not enough power in his iTARDS-device – or in himself, for I believe he was dying – to effect the transition across a full twelve-months. Three weeks short.' Scrooge sighed. 'Still, you're here now.'

'Yes, Ebeneezer, I have come,' replied the Spirit. His lips moved, silently, as if he were quickly counting something up. Then he added: 'Forsooth.'

Something about his visitor struck Scrooge. 'You *shine*, Spirit,' he said. 'When you open your mouth, light comes out. Light spills from your eyes. What is it? Whence does it come?'

'It is my brain, O Ebeneezer Scrooge,' replied the ghost.

'Your brain is – a lantern?'

'It shines with all the thoughts that have been thought. It beams with all the life that has been lived – for where *is* human life if not within the organelle of thought and feeling, here?'

The more he looked, the more the beautiful Scrooge thought the light. 'There is magic in the light,' he said, in a warbly voice.

'Indeed. And *this* is what the Zombies crave. As life feeds death, so they devour the seat of thought, the throne of passion and of love, home of all human hopes and dreams and fears. Now they have conquered, eh, wait a sec, er, *conqueréd* the future – so – they will devour the past, consume it whole. Mankind will never have existed here. The cold, outnumbering dead, will sojourn make beneath chaste stars for all eternity.'

'Gosh,' said Scrooge. 'That doesn't sound fun.'

'I am a Spiritus Mundi, the ghost of all that there has ever been on earth. I am Time, just as my brothers twain. And death is bound by Time, as all things are. Between the Zombies and myself exists but one sole lonely bulwark – and it is the future, all humanity and all th' accumulated minds of millions. But Scrooge – you've seen how mankind is undone.' The Spirit gestured; but Scrooge needed no reminding – the sound of Zombies thumping at the door downstairs punctuated everything that was said. 'And with humanity's defeat comes this dire fate: for Time itself will be devoured.'

The thought made Scrooge tremble. 'Can it be so, dread Spirit?'

'Time is the medium through which mankind moves, as a fish moves through the ocean's stream. If Time is drained away, humanity can no more live than cod could thrive upon the dry red deserts of Arabia. There is another force, implacable, that needs not Time – *resents* it and detests the way time lets life move and thrive and multiply. Death is one name for it. These Zombies are its soldiery. And you have been selected, Scrooge, to fight against this dire and monstrous power.'

'But I am the least heroic of souls!' declared Scrooge, with energy. 'Why should this burden have been set upon *my* shoulders?'

'The answer to that question is writ within the past, as all such answers are. It can be only read in future time, as all human destinies must be.'

'Right,' said Scrooge. Then: 'Wait. What does *that* mean?'

'It meaneth – um,' said the Spirit. He thought for a while. 'I'm sorry,' it said in a less poetically modulated voice. 'When

I get into this . . . uh, idiom, I can get a bit, you know. Carried away. It all gets a little, ah, *vatic* in my head. The flow can sort of overtake the sense, you know?' He coughed, looked nervously about, adding in a louder voice, as if for an unseen suitor, 'I come to you upon this Christmas Day—'

'Yes,' interrupted Scrooge. 'About that. *Why* can you only come on Christmas Day? I mean, I think I understand all the stuff about the Spiritus Mundi, and the embodiment of human thought, and the implacable dire power that sets itself against Time and everything. But none of that explains – why *Christmas*?'

The Spirit looked at the floor. Then, with a surreptitious glance about him, he glided over to Scrooge. 'It's complicated,' he said.

'I'm sure it is.'

'No, I mean,' he lowered his voice. 'It's complicated to fit it into iambic pentameters.'

'O K,' said Scrooge, uncertainly.

'I mean I'll *try* and fit it in. Obviously. It is, you know, expected of me. Yes? But you may need to bear with it, and not . . . you know,' he lowered his voice even further, almost to a whisper, 'be too *critical.*'

'I promise,' said Scrooge.

'O K then,' mouthed the Spirit.

At that exact moment, the door to the laboratory was beaten down, coming clean off its hinges and cracking hard against the floor. Scrooge jumped. The Spirit jumped. They both jumped. Actually the Spirit jumped a little higher, but apart from that they were pretty much as one.

Through the open door, into the moonlit room, came the lumbering form of a Zombie. Scrooge bolted, tripped over some of the junk littering the room and fell down hard. He got up hurriedly, but the creature was on him. The mephitic breath of the Zombie wafted right into his face as it bared its teeth: 'BRAAAINS!'

Scrooge's opinion of this new state of affairs was: 'Aaargh!'

Everything stopped.

Scrooge had closed his eyes, ready for the fatal bite. When it did not come, he opened his eyes again. The Zombie was in mid-lunge, its toenail-yellow teeth about to connect with the flesh of Scrooge's face. Its tongue was black like a slug. There was a gold filling in one tooth.

Scrooge looked to the ghost, who was holding up a wand of silver, narrow and short as a pencil. Sharp at one end too – indeed, it truly looked *like* a pencil. The Spirit twitched it, as an orchestral conductor might, and the Zombie closed its mouth and drew its head back.

'You can *control* them?' Scrooge gasped.

'Not exactly.'

The Zombie opened its mouth, and a sound emerged. 'SNEEAAA—' it moaned, weirdly, 'ARB!'

'Arb?' said Scrooge.

The Spirit waved his stick more rapidly, and the Zombie stepped backwards smartly through the doorway. The door shuddered upon the floor, leapt upright and fitted itself back into the frame. 'Behold the mystery of time reversed!' announced the Spirit in a loud voice. Then, more confidentially, he added: 'I'm going to waft us upwards, I think. Otherwise the reversal will tend to show us stuff that you, er, *don't* want to see. The cycle of eating and digestion, for instance, becomes an uncommonly *revolting* thing to watch in reverse.'

'Oh,' said Scrooge.

'Come to the window. We'll slide up the shaft of moonlight.'

Once again Scrooge was transported through time; but this experience was very different to the hoopy transmission that had brought him to the dawn of the twentieth century. There were no circles; but rather a mist that surrounded them both, glinting in the silver light of the moon, and roiling and uncurling in ways that seemed to defy the usual physics of such things. Every now and again snatches of sound, twisted and malformed, floated past Scrooge's ears: a strange stew of noises, some incomprehensible, some almost taking the form of sense.

'My brother Spirits have shown you the horror that begins in London Town – and shown you that it sweeps the world across,' said the Ghost of Christmas Past.

Scrooge put his hands before his face. 'The visions have changed me utterly!' he cried. 'Never again shall I cut myself off from humanity – I shall be a kind and tender-hearted man, if only I am restored to human society! I swear it!'

'Oh,' said the Spirit. 'For we were rather hoping that – you'll pardon me—'

'Yes?'

'That you would now – annihilate Tiny Tim.'

Scrooge thought about this. 'Annihilate?' he said.

'Kill, murder, bash his head through. Do him in.'

'You want my first act, in my new-found goodness of heart, to be the cold-blooded murder of a child?'

'No child he! His frame is small, skin smooth, because of scientific tweaking of the bodily expression of his genes. Only *technology* makes him seem young.'

'But even so! To . . . kill him?'

'You saw him stab my brother in the back?'

'I did,' said Scrooge.

The ghost was quiet for a space; and then spoke. 'This horror comes upon the world on Christmas Day.'

'Zombies, you mean?'

The ghost nodded.

'Zombies – of lesser potency it's true, but Zombies ne'er-theless – they came before as plagues upon your world. Before your time.'

'Yet the historical record—' Scrooge faltered. 'I mean, there is no mention—'

'It happened still, although it was contained. It scarred mankind's collective consciousness too deep to be recalled as "history". It is remembered now only as myth – but myth is true remembrance. Every year you re-enact the story yet again, though you've forgotten quite the origin of all your Christmas rituals and rites.'

Scrooge's mind seemed to gape. 'You are talking about – *Christmas*?'

'The word itself contains the memory of a time when graves spat horrors on the world, when Zombies swarmed the land, and mankind strove and fought to crush the mass of Zombiekind.'

'Crush Zomb-mass,' gasped Scrooge.

'Across the centuries,' agreed the Spirit, 'the word had been worn smooth in use, sea-smoothed as pebbles are – Chrzmbmas – Christmas.' The Spirit paused. 'Though history records not all the fear you faced down once upon a Christmas time, yet still your Christmas rituals record the truth. Yea, all your Yule traditions mark that time when the dead died not, when a tide of Zombies met contending with You-all.' He broke off, and added, sotto voce: 'I'll tell you, old bean: having light pouring from one's eyes is all very well and good, but it makes it ra-a-ather hard to see things yourself, you know, distinctly. Are you taking all this in?'

'I – yes. I think so.'

'You understand the iambs? Christmas records the original Zombie attack?'

'But,' said Scrooge. 'I had always been led to believe that the traditions of Christmas memorialise the birth of *Christ*?'

The Spirit straightened, assumed its vatic pose, and replied: 'Fir trees from northern European woods? What does such foliage have to do with Christ?' fluted the ghost. 'Hmm? Presents wrapped in boxes? Christmas *Puds*? What relevance do these have for the Biblical New Testament account?'

Scrooge shook his head. 'I do not know,' he answered.

'The reasons here are obvious enough,' said the Spirit. 'For what's a Christmas tree, in sooth, if not a living being wrenched-up from its soil, roots torn and broken and yet still alive – a tree that's forced to carry on inside a deathly half-life for twelve Christmas days? And what of giving presents. What is that?'

'It is, surely, simple gift-giving,' said Scrooge. 'Why is another explanation needful?'

'But think of this – for it has never been tradition that these gifts are simply *given*,' said the Spirit, the light flaring white from its eyes and mouth, the very hairs on its head conducting the light along its filaments and passing along the top of his head like sunlight over a cornfield. 'Rather each present must first be *interred* – put in a box, a model coffin – wrapped as in a shroud and then symbolically buried at the base of th' Christmas tree. Each gift is like a corpse, dead in the ground – until comes Christmas morning, when the dead, *un*buried, all come lumbering back to life . . .'

'I had not considered it in that light,' said Scrooge, doubtfully.

'Most everything about your Christmases recall the Zombie plague – *in allegory*. Torn limbs and broken bones –

just think about the severed feet you hang upon the end of all your children's beds on Christmas Eve! And Christmas Crackers? They're symbolic limbs you humans fight amongst yourselves to wrench asunder. And the Christmas pudding . . .'

'The Christmas *pudding*?' Scrooge objected.

'And have you *truly* never thought of it? Only at this time of year do people eat this special pudding. What does it encode? What symbolise? In texture, shape, deliciousness – fringed with blue flame that plays across it, evanescent, shining and as bright as any gleam of human thought. What else but *brain*?'

'Brain!'

'Yes. Brain. In sweetmeat form,' confirmed the Spirit. 'For at Yuletide, on that one day, all human kind enacts that which draws Zombies toward human life in the first place. Human chefs create a meal delicious to yourselves as brains are to the Zombie kind: the spongy texture, slightly granular, and moist with juice; sweet, spicy and alive. One day each year humanity does this. You never thought to wonder why you do?'

'You teach me, Spirit.'

'And what of Christmas carols, Mr Scrooge? Each year you chant them, singing words by rote and never thinking what they actually mean.'

'Do they actually mean Zombies, grave Spirit?'

'They do. *God Rest You Merry Gentlemen*? Why else command these men to take their rest, at Christmas most especially? Rest how? Well, rest in peace, the carol means; lie still beneath the ground and leave the quick alone. It truly is a minatory hymn, praying the dead stay dead. And Scrooge, you know the song that's called "The Twelve Days of Christmas"?'

'I know it,' said Scrooge.

'You never shuddered at its nightmare world?' asked the Spirit.

'Nightmare?'

'Those leaping lords – those drummers flailing arms? The Christmas landscape populated with these clustered ranks of twitching, jerking folk? What other scene do you think it describes?'

'Zombies!' gasped Scrooge. The mist around them seemed to be thinning, and Scrooge cast his eyes about. But everything was still murk. 'But Spirit,' he pressed, urgently. 'Why *Christmas*?'

The Spirit's light was growing brighter, and seemed to spill and pool upon the mist that surrounded them. 'My time with you is coming to an end,' he said.

'No, Spirit! Do not leave me! Can you not answer that one question? There is some magic in Christmas – something about this day that gives force and endurance to the Zombie plague. Why? Why Christmas Day! I understand that Timh has come back to this time – *my* time – and has laboured to spread the Zombie plague. But not until Christmas Day itself does the plague break out. What is the magic of that date?'

The mist was dispersing. Scrooge found himself standing upon a cobbled street. It was dark.

'You have returned to where you started from. It is now Christmas Eve,' said the Spirit. 'There is still time. But do not tarry here ... though Timh was weakened by his accident, and though it is not *yet* – quite – Christmas Day, the threshold when his power can flow undimmed, yet time won't wait—'

The brightness was drawing back, as cloth is folded and tucked into pleats: distilling, or congealing, into patches and revealing darkness in between – and then shrinking further into blobs of light. Scrooge gasped and looked about, and saw that he was in a street, at night, not far from his place of work. The light was now only a string of gas-light lanterns, at the top of metal poles, and casting a slick light upon the cobblestones below. 'Spirit?' Scrooge cried. 'Spirit?'

He looked about him, and he was alone in the street.

It did not take him long to get his bearings. He was truly back in London – in the Aldwych; on a foggy and bitterly cold night. He recognised the street: behind him, the bridge; before, the narrow alleys and rookeries of the poor. His own chambers were not far: a little way along the Strand. There was nobody about.

But, wait: there *was* somebody – a thin man wrapped in greatcoat and comforter, his head down and his steps determined, marching along the Strand, passing from pool of light to pool of light. It took a moment for him to recognise the figure.

'Scrooge!' he called out, as much in astonished recognition as in greeting. 'Ebeneezer Scrooge!'

The other Scrooge stopped, and turned. The sourness of his face was apparent even at this distance, even in this fog: a pinched, wary, unpleasant screwedupness of countenance. Scrooge felt his innards shift about, as if a mighty ocean tide were turning: he *remembered* this moment – it was Christmas Eve, and he was hurrying home. The encounter with Marley's Zombie was yet to come! The Spirit had shown him the past! But with a secondary inner shock Scrooge bethought himself: he heard me! I called to him and he *heard* my call. He was no mere bystander here.

In the excitement of comprehension, Scrooge began waving his arms. 'Scrooge!'

The earlier version of himself paused, turned and took a few steps towards him.

'Scrooge!' Scrooge yelled. 'Beware!'

'Begone sir,' the other replied, in a voice filled with rage. 'Go on your way.'

'Beware of *Marley*!' Scrooge cried. Shudders chased one another up and down his body – for he was in the night-time chill and wearing nothing but a nightgown. His voice began to trip over his chattering teeth. Should he let it go? After all, he had defeated the Zombie Marley, had he not? But then a worm of doubt crawled through Scrooge's thoughts: had his return, in time, altered things? Did this alter-ego face a fight he might lose? If so, he had a clear duty to try and warn his earlier self against the attack he knew was coming. He called at Scrooge to arm himself with a poker, as soon as he got home. Then, his disordered thoughts coming back to him, he added: 'Your gold! That will save you!'

The earlier version of Scrooge looked most ferociously at him. Scrooge ran a few steps towards himself, and began – in a rather hurried, almost gabbling manner – to explain how Marley was to be defeated. The gold bar, the drawer from the chest, the poker ... but the problem was that so much had happened since his first encounter with a Zombie, and the shock of that encounter had jumbled up his memory, so that he was not entirely coherent in what he said. The more he spoke the more hostile and contemptful his earlier self became.

Indeed, the earlier version of Scrooge soon interrupted, gesticulating and shouting. Scrooge was shaking so with the cold, and the blood was thundering in his ears to such a degree, that he barely heard. 'Go!' the earlier version of himself cried. 'You know where to go! ... Comes to me ... *Cratchit*!'

The words went through Scrooge's mind like a sword.

Of course! Cratchit – he couldn't allow himself to be distracted like this. He had to get to the Cratchits' house. There wasn't a moment to lose. The Cratchits lived in Southwark. The words of the Ghost of Christmas Past returned to him. Hurry!

He turned and started across the bridge.

The tollbooth – usually occupied at all times – was empty. Presumably the tollman was away enjoying a tot of rum. Perhaps more than a tot – maybe a whole toot.

Scrooge was enough himself to be grateful for this small detail; for in his nightgown as he was he carried not money. And he needed to get to the Surrey bank of the river without delay.

He ran as fast as his legs would carry him. On either side the invisible river, upon the surface of which flowed a ghostly secondary river of fog, hushed him. Gaslights, each isolated from its pole by the fog, hovered like spirit-lanterns at regular intervals all the way over. 'Cratchit, Cratchit ...' Scrooge gasped, as he ran.

At the far end of the bridge Scrooge passed into Southwark, and into darkness. He was too desperate even to be afraid.

He ran hard as he could through the dark streets, and all the way he asked himself, over and over: did he have the strength of purpose to kill Timh? He knew everything that was at stake – he had witnessed the future with his own eyes. If murdering this one individual would prevent all that misery, and save the entirety of the planet, was he not morally *obligated* to perform the action? And *yet*, and *yet* (those two words repeated over and over in Scrooge's mind to the rhythm of his feet slapping the cobbles) – and yet, to *kill* another human being, in cold blood? What if his courage failed at the last minute?

He passed a knot of carol singers; their song seemed to clatter in his ear, distorted by his own panting breath – *Sing, Zom, Merrily On High*. He turned a corner and had to stop to catch his breath. No longer a young man, he thought, putting his hand against a wall for balance. Not as strong as once he was. The carol singers had started a new song, muffled by the distance and the fog and barely audible.

> *CHECK the halls for crowds of Zombies*
> *'Larm! Alarm! Alarm! A-larm, a-larm!*

'It's monstrous!' he gasped. 'Monstrous!' He forced his aching legs into a run. He had to hurry – he had to get to the Cratchits' house. He had to kill Ni Timh. His feet slapped and stumbled on the pavement: and *yet*, and *yet*, and *yet*.

And here he was. The Cratchits had no bell, so he pummelled on the door with his fists, barely able to gasp out 'Open up! Open up!'

It took several minutes; but his clerk eventually opened it, with a candle in his hand. 'Why Mr Scrooge!' he exclaimed, surprised. 'What brings you down here!'

Scrooge pushed past the fellow and barged into the house. 'Cratchit,' he said. 'There's no time to lose!'

'To lose what, sir?' asked Cratchit, following him down the narrow little hall.

'Tim,' said Scrooge. 'You must take me to Tim!'

'What – little Tim? Our adopted boy?'

'He. The entire future of humanity depends upon it!'

'He's down in the parlour,' said Cratchit, in a puzzled voice. 'We all are. It'll be midnight in a little while – and Christmas Day.'

Scrooge got to the end of the narrow hall and burst into the parlour. The whole family was gathered there: Mrs Cratchit, looking up from some darning. Little George and Georgina, and littlest Georgia. And there, in a miniature chair in the corner, with his crutches balanced against the side, was Timh – looking as diminutive, and ill, and puffy-faced, and helpless as ever a cripple child did. '*You!*' Scrooge cried, pointing. '*You!*'

'I?' wheezed Timh, looking surprised.

'You!'

'He?' asked Cratchit nervously.

'He!'

'Who?' asked Mrs Cratchit.

'He!'

'You?' said Cratchit, looking at his adopted son.

'You!' confirmed Scrooge, looking in the same direction.

'I?' said Timh, again.

'Ni!' growled Scrooge.

'What?' interjected Cratchit.

Scrooge turned to explain what must be done – to tell these people why he had come. But the sight stopped him in his tracks: the innocent little family scene – it possessed a charm and a sanctity to touch even the chilliest of hearts. Could he really violate this little scene – this humble candlelit parlour, the children's shining faces awaiting Christmas, the patient long-suffering mother, the humble father? Could he murder the smallest member of this family in cold blood? He turned back to the evil mastermind who had either brought so much misery upon the world, or else would bring so much misery upon the world, depending on the complexity of the time-lines.

'If I didn't know better,' Scrooge said to Timh, although in a wavering voice. 'If I didn't know better I might believe you actually *were* a disfigured and crippled child, Timh.'

'What do you say, sir?' piped Timh, ingenuously.

'Don't play games with me, Ni,' Scrooge scowled. 'I know your true identity!'

'Mr Scrooge,' said Cratchit, stepping between his employer and his adopted son. 'What are you saying, sir? *What* true identity?'

'Ni!'

'Ni?'

'Ni! Ni!'

Timh looked at his knee.

Over by the table, Mrs Cratchit said, in an uncertain voice, 'Nini?'

'You embodiment of evil!' cried Scrooge.

'I'm sorry, Mr Scrooge,' Cratchit put in. 'You may be my employer – but you're a guest in my house, and you'll have to be more civil than that.'

Scrooge looked into the man's face. It was worn with exhaustion and bore the unmistakable signs of sickness. Sweat stood upon his brow.

'You are ill, sir,' said Scrooge, recoiling a little.

'There is some low fever in the house,' conceded Cratchit. 'We all have it. But it is not serious. A mere sniffle. Really, not more than a little sinus pain and a *slightly* runny nose.' He smiled at Scrooge, weakly. Then he fell forward to land, face downwards, on the parlour floor.

Scrooge bent down. 'Cratchit? What's wrong?'

But Terence Cratchit was dead.

Scrooge looked up, wildly. 'He was sick? Sick with a fever? I fear he was much more sickly than he realised?'

'Terence?' said Mrs Cratchit, in a wobbly voice. She put her darn down, and said. 'Mr Scrooge, has my husband fainted?'

'Mrs Cratchit,' said Scrooge. 'I regret to inform you that—'

But before he could finish the sentence, Mrs Cratchit pitched forward out of her chair and fell hard as a dropped sack of grain upon the tiles of the parlour floor. She lay beside her husband, unbreathing.

'*Both* dead?' cried Scrooge. 'What miasma of death is here? Children! Children!'

The three youngsters leapt from their chairs, bouncy and excited. 'Sir!' they yipped. 'Mr Scrooge, sir!' 'Do you bring us Christmas presents, sir?' lisped the youngest.

'Children, we must all quit this place, lest the contagion . . .'

The eldest child flopped over to lie motionless.

'Ah, well – you two at any rate. I'll take you to . . .'

The next one fell over.

'Right, right. I'm going to stop talking, little Georgie, and just take you straight out to a hospital . . .'

The last fell forward.

Scrooge surveyed the pile of unbreathing bodies. 'OK,' he said, shortly. 'Right.'

'Just you and me, now, old Scroogie,' said Timh, from his chair, his voice changed.

'So,' said Timh. 'You tracked me down – came to stop me, eh? So you arrive *on the very eve of my triumph*!'

'It has been given to me to stop you,' Scrooge confirmed. 'Though it be a painful duty.'

'You will – what?' said Timh, sneeringly. '*Batter* me to death with my own crutches? Kill a little crippled child on Christmas Eve?'

'You are no child,' said Scrooge, firmly. 'I do not know *what* you are – but you are not that.'

'You don't know me, Scrooge,' said Timh. 'But I know you. I know what you are capable of doing – and murdering me is not one of those things.'

Scrooge felt a spurt of fury in his breast. He leapt forward, snatched up one of Timh's crutches – the idea having been put in his head – and brandished it like a sword. 'Don't taunt me, Ni – see? – or so help me I'll . . .'

Timh sat in his chair looking up at Scrooge expectantly. 'Yes?'

It was no good. Scrooge could not do it. Still holding the crutch he sat down in a vacant chair beside the parlour table. 'It's too much to ask of any man,' he muttered.

'Of course it is,' said Timh, in a pleasant voice. 'You're no killer. And besides, we're old friends. You can't be expected to murder an old friend! How well I remember our last chat, in that house in Perth!'

'How did you come to be here?' Scrooge demanded.

A shadow of wrath passed over Timh's face. 'That Spirit friend of yours – he caused me significant . . . inconvenience. His device was charged to explode. I travelled through time – though lamed and broken by the temporal explosion. And arrived in London a few years ago – not where or when I was aiming to be. And I certainly hoped to arrive in better physical condition. In fact I was so injured that it was all I could manage to stagger to the Cratchits' front door. They took pity on me, these poor kind-hearted saps. Gave me a home – thinking me an orphan child scorched in some disaster. They adopted me, and tended me as best they could. Little did they know!'

'And this,' said Scrooge, gesturing at the bodies of the family lying upon the floor, 'is how they are repaid?'

'Naturally I brought with me, from the future,' said Timh, 'a phial containing my brilliant new distillation of the Zombie plague: a new mutation. I'd been working upon it in the laboratory for years. You see, in its natural form – in the form in which it entered the world, that Christmas, long ago – the plague is passed to human carriers only with great difficulty. It was much easier to contain. But I used all my knowledge to engineer a *new* strain – one *much* more virulent.'

'But *why*? Why have you done this?' cried Scrooge. 'To loose such misery upon the world!'

'Let us sit together,' said Timh, pleasantly. 'Let us see in Christmas Day together. What you need to understand is that it is inevitable – it has always been inevitable, ever since that first Christmas brought this into the world.'

'The first Christmas?' repeated Scrooge.

'Do you still not understand? Whence comes the Zombie plague? Did your Spirit friends not explain?'

'They told me that Christmas Day possesses some potency – that the plague could not be loosed upon any other day.'

'And did you think to wonder why?'

'The Ghost of Christmas Past said that our Christmas rituals memorialised a previous outbreak of the plague . . .'

'Not an outbreak,' said Timh, sitting forward in his miniature chair, his eyes bright. 'The outbreak. The first Christmas!'

Scrooge felt a sense of discomfort crawling in his belly, as if he were on the edge of a blasphemy. 'I'll not believe it, Timh . . .' he cried. 'Do not tell me that – do not tell me that . . .'

'Tell you what, Ebeneezer Scrooge?'

'That Christ was a . . .' The word refused to emerge.

'Oh you've got the *wrong* end of the stick, Scrooge,' said

Ni, his voice thin but forceful. 'Christ was no Zombie. *His* coming brought life into the world. But Ebeneezer Scrooge – *you* know that the world exists in a balance – that nothing is given without something being taken away; that everything has its cost, equal and opposite. When life came into the world there was a cost. That cost was death.'

'I don't follow. Surely death was already in the world?'

'Have you travelled through time to the end of humanity, and back again to your own time, you silly man, without comprehending that there is more than one manner of death? There is the death at the end of life, the death of fullness as natural as winter coming after summer. But then there is another form of death: a hungry death, a death that walks as a beast of prey, on two legs, hungry to devour life in its very source. Christ's coming, because it focused a new point of Life, Eternal Life, in the world, *upset the equilibrium of things*. And so at that exact moment there came into being a point of Death, Eternal Death.'

Scrooge was shaking his head; and yet he found himself believing what he was hearing. His whole life of buying and selling, of negotiating deals upon the Exchange – but more than that, his observations about pain and pleasure in life; about reward and loss; about virtue and vice – all told him that the world was a balance. How could the entry of a being such as Christ not upset that balance? How could the equal-and-opposite reaction of the cosmos to something so monumental as the Nativity not entail the most profound, and disturbing, possibilities.

'You are so used to viewing the Nativity from the point of view of a mortal,' said Timh, 'that you have never taken the trouble to see it as a god would see it. To abdicate *immortality* and take on *mortality* – to slip *into* death, like putting on a robe stitched of corpses. Imagine it! From cleanness into uncleanness. The nearest equivalent, for a mortal, would be to step from your life into the life-in-death of a Zombie.'

'Yet you said,' put in Scrooge, 'that Christ was no Zombie . . .'

'Two beings came into the world at that moment,' said Timh, a gleam in his eyes. 'One was called Christ, and spread Life through the world in the form of the Word . . . for words are life. That is why my poor Zombies cannot speak – or can but barely utter clumsy words. The Other spread Death through the world as a plague. From time to time in human affairs this plague has broken forth – but never, until this moment, has it had the necessary force to spread as it ought to.'

'Yet if the plague has come before, and has been defeated before—' said Scrooge, sitting upright in his chair, hope in his voice. 'Then it can be defeated again!'

'Defeated – yes it was. That first time. But at some cost. You've heard of the Massacre of the Innocents,' said Timh, in a gloaty voice. 'You know it is forever associated with Christmas, and yet you have never pondered why?'

'I had always been taught that Herod,' said Scrooge, 'Herod, in his wrath, was trying to murder the Christ child . . .'

'The story has economised upon the complexity of events,' said Timh. 'That's how legends work. For three days the Zombie plague was passed about the countryside. Jerusalem was plagued with monsters – devouring the brains of Jew and Gentile both, of Roman and Native. Herod was king, and did not know what to do. I don't think he would have done anything, either, if your three friends hadn't come to advise him.'

'My three friends?'

'The Spirits. Your ghostly pals. I believe, in accounts of those things, they're called the Magi.'

Scrooge's jaw fell upon his chest. 'I,' he gasped. 'I didn't realise.'

'Indeed. So Herod sent the army out: killed a lot of children. A lot of men and women too, but it's the children that legend remembers. And that's the situation *you* find yourself in, eh Scrooge? Kill a child, and prevent the plague. Go down in history as a new Herod. Are you prepared to do that?'

Scrooge stared fiercely at the little being. Timh met and returned his gaze without flinching.

'No,' said Timh, in a quieter voice. 'I didn't think so.'

Distantly, through the cold and the fog and the dark, the sound of Southwark Cathedral bells came tolling: one, two three. Scrooge leapt to his feet.

'Christmas Day!'

'And now,' said Timh, smiling, 'it is too late.' He laughed, a brief, ugly, triumphant laugh. It was not a laugh that tinkled *ha-ha-ha*! It began with a *bw*.

Four. Five. Six.

'I have infected those I could,' said Timh. 'Those who have been in this house, with me,' said Timh. 'Alas that I have been too crippled to venture abroad. But it is enough! My dear adopted family, in its entirety – and Marley, too, of course, who visited so assiduously on his charitable trips out. They are all infected with the new strain.'

Seven, eight, nine.

'Marley I sent on a particular task – to kill you, Ebeneezer. Because you are the only person to carry the immunity. That you are immune is not a serious difficulty, I believe; humanity will not have the wit to make a serum against the plague until it is much too late. I have seen the future, you know. But I wanted to make assurance double sure.'

Ten, eleven, twelve.

It was Christmas Day.

'The Cratchits,' Timh went on, 'had an easier task: simply to spread the virulent new form as widely as possible. And they have bustled hither and yon, over the last few days. The focus of magical force Christmas Day entails would be enough to establish the plague in the general population. After that, I can let nature take its course.'

On the floor of the parlour, the bodies of the two adults and the three children were beginning to twitch. Moans emerged from the mass.

'Uh-oh,' said Scrooge.

'I was able to keep you talking,' said Timh, delightedly. 'Talking and listening – to delay you until Christmas Day begins. You fool! You should have struck when you had the chance! It's too late now! Your tender little conscience has doomed all your kind! Humanity will be consumed by the Zombie plague! My victory is compl– *Ugh.*'

Scrooge had struck him on the top of the head with the crutch.

'Ow,' said Timh. 'Steady on!'

Scrooge hit him again.

Timh's eyes went cross-y, as if he were trying to bring the tip of his nose into focus. 'Ooo,' he said.

Scrooge brought the crutch down a third time, and with all his might. Timh's head lolled forward.

All around him corpses were stirring. 'Time,' Scrooge said, aloud, 'to get out of here.'

As he turned to the parlour's one door Cratchit popped up. His iteration of the inevitable word, when it came, was rather higher-pitched than Scrooge had become used to. But it was unmistakable for all that: 'Braains!'

'Eek,' replied. Scrooge. He hit at the creature with the

crutch, but he might as well have been striking a lamp post.

The Zombie-Cratchit flailed with his arms, and sank his nails into Scrooge's shoulders. Roaring, he opened his mouth wide and jabbed forward – Scrooge, acting instinctively, thrust up with the crutch he was holding, interposing it between his attacker and his own vulnerable face. There was a small nodule of india-rubber on the tip of the crutch, and instead of biting into Scrooge's nose, Cratchit-Zombie set his teeth about this. With all his strength Scrooge thrust the crutch. Cratchit's head went back, so Scrooge – encouraged – performed a second crutch-thrust, and then a third. He broke away, and staggered back a few steps.

'Braaai—' Cratchit's Zombie began to roar, but the india-rubber plug had come off the bottom of the crutch inside his mouth, and now he appeared to have inhaled it. He coughed, made a sort of clucking, squawking noise. Scrooge gaped. Presumably the thing did not need to breath – what with being dead, and everything – but at the least, the presence of a large chunk of india-rubber in his windpipe was preventing him from shouting about brains.

The rest of the family were starting to stir. Scrooge looked about him: soon enough he would be faced with a roomful of Zombies. He needed to get out, and there was only one door.

But as he turned to this, the youngest Cratchit – Georgie – hopped onto the table, squeaked 'braains!' in a childish voice, and leapt through the air at Scrooge.

Scrooge acted without thought – whipped up the crutch, sans india-rubber plug, to ward off the attack. The end caught Georgie in the middle of the chest, and the impact of even so small an individual knocked Scrooge back. He was able – just – to push back so that the Zombie-infant pivoted upon this point and was deflected from him. Georgie flew towards the kitchen, and landed head-first in the Christmas Pudding that Mrs Cratchitt had prepared. The pudding, being larger than his head, swallowed the infant's cranium completely.

Terence Cratchit was lumbering towards him. 'Kh!' he croaked. 'Kkhh!'

Scrooge tried to bring the crutch round again, but tripped instead over the groaning, trembling body of Mrs Cratchit and went down on all fours. He scrambled forward, and got up again just in time to avoid young Georgie, who had stumbled out of the kitchen area with a pudding for a head.

Cratchit finally expelled the india-rubber plug with a 'kh-kk[*poing*]RAINS!' He seemed delighted, in a Zombic way, to be able to yell again. 'Brains! Brains! Brains!'

The plug shot across the room, caught the candlestick dead centre and knocked it clean over.

The candle flew free, and landed, flame-side down, upon the pudding-head of young Georgie.

Soaked in brandy as it was, the pudding mixture instantly caught alight.

'Braains!' cried Zombie-Cratchit. His Zombified child blundered against him, setting fire to his shirt.

'Braains!' cried Mrs Cratchit, from the floor.

'Merry Christmas,' said Scrooge, stepping smartly into the hall and shutting the parlour door behind him.

There was no lock, and precious little furniture with which to jam the door shut. But there was a small chair placed underneath the stairway, and Scrooge wedged this as best he could beneath the handle. The Zombies inside the parlour were thumping at the wood on the far side.

Scrooge slipped through the front door, being sure to take the key from the inside lock so that he could lock the portal behind him. He essayed one last glance back, just as a Zombie fist smashed through one of the panels of the parlour door. One glance was enough: the room beyond was now completely on fire; a small figure with a flaming pudding for a head staggered from right to left; the undead figure of his former clerk tore at the wood in his own door.

Scrooge shut the front door, and locked it.

He made his way into the middle of the road, and looked back. Flames from the back of the house were visible, staining the fog orange. Soon the whole structure would be on fire – there was every chance the blaze would spread to the surrounding houses too.

He had to warn the occupants of those houses. Then, with a piercing clarity, he realised: he had to warn the whole city! Who knew how many people had been infected with the Zombie plague by the Cratchits? But it was not too late . . . He, Scrooge, knew enough now to be able to rally Londoners in the fight against this peril. Ni Timh was dead, and could not coordinate the assault. All that remained was to make sure that every Zombie to appear was killed. Again.

'People of London!' Scrooge bellowed, into the night sky. 'Heed me! We are under attack from a terrible foe, but I have the knowledge to save us! Let us remember the true meaning of Christmas, and crush the Zombie mass. To you all I say: GO BASH 'EM, EVERY ZOM!'